QUITTING
TIME

QUITTING

TIME

ROBERT J. CONLEY

M. EVANS
Lanham • Boulder • New York • Toronto • Plymouth, UK

Published by M. Evans
An imprint of Rowman & Littlefield
4501 Forbes Boulevard, Suite 200, Lanham, Maryland 20706
www.rowman.com

10 Thornbury Road, Plymouth PL6 7PP, United Kingdom

Distributed by National Book Network

British Library Cataloguing in Publication Information Available

Library of Congress Cataloging-in-Publication Data

The hardback edition of this book was previously cataloged by the Library of
Congress as follows:

Conley, Robert J.
  Quitting Time / Robert J. Conley.
    p. cm. — (An Evans novel of the West)
  I. Title. II. Series.
  PS3553.0494Q58   1989
  813'.54—dc20

ISBN: 978-1-59077-410-6 (pbk. : alk. paper)
ISBN: 978-1-59077-411-3 (electronic)

Printed in the United States of America

Chapter One

Colfax meant to get drunk. It was a new development in his life, but in his late forties almost everything about his life had changed. He had spent several productive years, if such they could be called, as a professional gunman, a killer for hire. It was true that he had operated during those years by means of a peculiarly personal ethical code. He had believed that all men were depraved and therefore worthy of death, and each time he took on a new job, he had studied his prey until he had managed to convince himself that this particular individual did indeed support his belief. That way he had the comfort of both his generalized philosophy that no man deserved to live and the individual corroborations of the credo.

It had worked just fine until he had met Luton. He had taken on the job of killing Luton, and he had put his usual practice into motion. He had met Luton, stalked him, watched for Luton to make a wrong move, reveal his tragic flaw, his secret depravity. It hadn't worked. Colfax had wound up convinced that Luton was a good man. Its philosophical basis shattered, Colfax's career came to an abrupt halt. He had eventually taken on new jobs, but he had been much more selective about them. He had served as bodyguard to people who were being threatened. He had helped run down known and wanted criminals. But the jobs were few and far between.

Colfax was a man alone, with no place to go and nothing to look forward to. He still had some money, though the bank account was getting low, and he saw no immediate means of replenishing it. He was thinking that he would have to make some changes in his life, move out of the city and the expensive hotel in which he had been staying, go someplace different, find a new way of making a living. But first he would get drunk.

He was sitting at a table alone in a dark corner of the hotel lounge, a bottle of Courvoisier there before him and a snifter in his hand, when he saw the stranger walk toward him. He knew the man was coming in his direction as there was no one else on that side of the room. He had seen the man come into the lounge and stop at the bar, had noticed the cowboy clothes and pegged the man for a rancher come to town on business. He had seen the cowboy speak to the bartender, but all that had just been casual observation. He had not really been watching, had not been concerned. Now the man was walking deliberately toward him. Colfax's old reflexes caused him to reach down to feel the handle of the big Colt which was riding just to the right of his navel. The cowboy came closer. Colfax relaxed a little as he realized that the cowboy was not carrying a gun, at least not one that showed, and that he was carrying in his right hand a folded newspaper. Colfax tossed down the brandy in his snifter and leaned back in his chair. The cowboy stopped a few feet away from the table and took off his hat.

"Mr. Colfax?" he said.

Colfax stared at the stranger for a long moment.

"I'm Colfax," he said.

"Oliver Colfax?"

"That's right."

"My name is Boyd Gruver. I work for Mr. Tiff Lanagan who's got a big spread out in Colorado."

Colfax had heard of Lanagan, one of the western cattle barons, but he chose to remain silent and hear what Gruver had to say.

"Mr. Lanagan sent me to look you up with a proposition," said Gruver. "All right if I set down and talk?"

Colfax poured himself another snifter of brandy and gestured toward the chair directly across the table from where he sat.

"Sit," he said.

Gruver pulled out the chair and sat down.

"Mr. Colfax," he said, "my boss would like to hire you."

"I'm not a cowpuncher," said Colfax, "and I'm too old to start a new trade."

"Mr. Colfax, no offense, but Mr. Lanagan knows what your trade is."

Colfax didn't like Gruver. His eyes narrowed as he looked across the table at the younger man.

"And just what is that trade, sonny?" he asked.

Gruver stiffened and his ears reddened slightly.

"Mr. Colfax," he said, "you're well known throughout the West as a, shall we say, enforcer? Mr. Lanagan needs someone with your abilities. He's prepared to pay the highest price."

"Does he want me to commit murder for him?"

"No," said Gruver. "No, I wouldn't call it that."

He looked nervous. He began to fidget in his chair, and he turned around and looked toward the bartender and made a wild gesture with his arm. The bartender came over to the table in a short while.

"Can I help you, sir?" he said.

"Bring me a bottle of Kentucky whiskey," said Gruver.

"Any brand?"

"Yeah. I don't care."

The bartender turned and headed back for the bar. Gruver avoided looking at Colfax. He took a small cigar out of his pocket and lit it. Colfax watched him the whole time with apparent disinterest.

"Gruver," said Colfax.

Gruver jumped slightly.

"Gruver, just what is this job that your boss wants me to do?"

"Well, you gotta understand, Mr. Colfax," said Gruver, "that Mr. Lanagan has been on his spread for a long time. He moved in there when the goddamned Indians was still running wild."

"I seriously question," said Colfax, "who was wild in that situation, but go on with your story."

"Well," said Gruver, "recently a new group has moved into the valley. A man named Larkin Wheeler has moved in. Brought a bunch of cows and a couple of cowboys."

"It's open range, isn't it?" said Colfax. "Nothing wrong with that."

"Yeah," said Gruver. "It's open range, all right. But Wheeler's shoving our cows off the range. He's brought in gunfighters. We don't have nothing but a bunch of cowboys. Professional gunfighters is too much of a match for us. What we got on our hands, Mr. Colfax, is the beginnings of a real range war."

Colfax turned down the contents of his snifter and poured it full again. He looked Gruver straight in the eyes.

"And you—or your boss, to be more precise—wants me to come in and kill off—or run off—the opposition. Is that right?"

"Well," said Gruver, "that's putting it pretty blunt, but I guess that's about what it amounts to. Yeah."

The bartender showed up and placed a bottle of whiskey and a glass in front of Gruver. While Gruver dug into his pockets to pay for the bottle, Colfax reached into his pockets for the makings of a cigarette. He calmly poured the tobacco into a paper and rolled it. As he licked the rolled cigarette, the bartender was walking away. Colfax struck a wooden match on the underside of the table and lit his cigarette.

"Gruver," he said, "I stopped killing for hire some years ago. I'm real particular these days who I hire out to. I don't know enough about your story to know which side is right and which one is wrong, and there's nothing you can say to convince me one way or the other. Whatever you say is going to be from the Lanagan point of view. You're going to tell me whatever the hell you know your boss wants you to tell me. Forget it."

4

"I didn't know you were so goddamned particular," said Gruver.

Colfax tossed down his brandy.

"Boy," he said, "I'm going to let that pass. You just go back to Colorado and tell your boss that old Colfax wasn't interested. Tell him the old man is rich and doesn't need any more money. Tell him that I've lost my nerve. Tell him any goddamned thing you want to tell him in order to save your job, but just get the hell out of here and leave me alone."

Gruver's ears reddened again. He kicked back his chair and stood up all in one motion, pulling a Smith & Wesson Pocket .32 out of somewhere and had it about halfway up to level.

"Damn you," he began, but Colfax's big Colt was leveled at his chest and he froze in position.

"Put that toy back in your pocket," said Colfax, "and get the hell out of here. Leave me in peace, the way you found me. I really don't want to kill anyone tonight."

Gruver slowly lowered the .32 and let it slip back into his side coat pocket. Then he held his hands out to his sides. He had been bested by a long ways, and he knew it. His face had turned gray, ashen, and he was trembling slightly.

"Mr. Colfax," he said in a quavering voice, "look, I'm sorry. I shouldn't have tried that. I'm sorry. My boss has an offer for you. It's a fair offer. No, more than that. It's a good offer. It could set you up for life, Mr. Colfax. I ain't lying to you. All right, maybe you got some scruples about who you work for. I don't know nothing about that. But there's a story in that newspaper there about what's been going on in our valley. You read that. You read that, and it'll tell you about what's been going on. You don't have to take my word for it. Read that paper, and I'll come back in the morning to see you. Okay?"

Colfax studied Gruver's face for a bit, then eased down the hammer of his Colt. He dropped the Colt back into its holster, which was strapped high on his waist and practically in the middle of his belly, never taking his eyes off Gruver.

"All right, Gruver," he said. "Leave your paper here, and I'll read it. I'll have breakfast here in the morning with you. Eight o'clock. Right here. On your boss. No promises. I'll talk to you in the morning. Now get out of here and leave me alone."

"I'll be here," said Gruver, and he turned and left the lounge without another word. Colfax poured himself another brandy. He wasn't quite drunk yet, and he remembered that his intention for the evening was to get that way. Then he reached across the table and dragged the folded newspaper over beside his drink.

"Son of a bitch," he mumbled.

Then he opened the paper to reveal the entire front page. There was the story that Gruver had referred to. The headlines blared out at him.

LOCAL RANCHERS THREATENED BY RUSTLERS AND SQUATTERS.

Colfax squinted his eyes and forced them to focus on the small print.

"Our valley," the article read, "is being threatened by an invasion. Rustlers and squatters have been moving in in droves and threatening the established economy of our community. Streams which flow through the open range, which belong to all of us, have been dammed and otherwise diverted, cattle have disappeared from the established herds of some of our most respected citizens, and squatters' cabins are beginning to blot the landscape in every direction. Tiff Lanagan, one of the pioneers of this valley, has told this reporter that his losses in the past six months have been heavy, indeed. All our livelihoods, all our welfare is at stake here. Something must be done, and done fast, if life as we know it in this valley is to continue. The safety of our wives and children is at stake. Capitalism, free enterprise, and the American way is being threatened. Something must be done and done soon."

Colfax snorted at the article and tossed down his brandy. Then, absentmindedly, he turned the page. Another headline caught his attention.

ADRIAN CHANNING TROUP TO PERFORM SHAKESPEARE HERE.

Colfax read on eagerly.

"On its tour of the western states, the famed Adrian Channing Shakespearean company of actors will stop here to perform the Bard's tragedy *Titus Andronicus*. Mr. Channing himself will portray Titus, and the acclaimed actress Alma Dyer will play Lavinia."

Colfax raced through the remainder of the article, which gave names of a few other members of the company and specific dates for the performances. He smacked his hand down on the table.

"Damn," he said out loud. "Goddamn. Titus. Nobody plays Titus. *Titus Andronicus*. Damn."

Gruver was waiting when Colfax showed up for breakfast. He stood up politely as Colfax approached the table.

"Good morning, sir. Did you read the paper?"

"After we eat, sonny," said Colfax. He waved an arm toward the waiter, then sat down in the same chair he had been in the night before. Then Gruver sat back down again. The waiter hurried over to the table.

"My usual," said Colfax. "And put it on his bill."

Gruver ordered ham and eggs, biscuits and gravy and coffee, and the waiter hustled away to set the breakfast in motion. He returned shortly with the coffee. Gruver took a sip, then put his cup back down.

"This Saint Looie's quite a town," he said.

"Your first visit?" asked Colfax.

"Yes, sir. I was real surprised when Mr. Lanagan sent me. Course, the way things are going back home, I know he didn't feel like he could just up and take off. Still, I never thought that he'd send me way out here on an errand like this. Hell, I'm just a cowpuncher."

There followed a long and uncomfortable period of silence in which the two men sipped their cups of coffee. Soon the waiter returned with two plates, a bowl of gravy, and a dish of biscuits.

"Dig in," said Colfax, and not another word was said until the meal was finished and the waiter had cleared away the dishes.

Then Colfax rolled a cigarette and lit it. He took a deep drag and expelled the smoke, then leaned back in his chair.

"You got a telegraph office out there where you live?" he said.

"Yes, sir." said Gruver.

Colfax reached inside his jacket and pulled out the newspaper that Gruver had left for him the night before. He tossed it on the table in front of Gruver, folded to the second-page story of the traveling Shakespeareans.

"I want to see that play," he said. "Here's my offer. You wire your boss and say that if he'll pay for my railroad ticket out there and back and buy me a ticket to that play, I'll come out and talk to him about his problems. There's no guarantee that I'll take the job after I've talked with him. That's it. That's my offer. He can take it or leave it. When you get his answer, you'll find me right here."

Gruver stood up hesitantly. He turned to leave the room, then turned back again as if he'd like to say something. Colfax pointed to the bill which the waiter had left on the table.

"Take that with you," he said. "And leave a decent tip on the table."

Gruver tossed some coins on the table and picked up the bill.

"Mr. Colfax," he said, "did you read the article in the paper that I showed you."

"Boy," said Colfax, "that damned newspaper didn't tell me any more about the situation out there than you did. Your boss is undoubtedly the biggest rancher in those parts."

"Yes, sir, he is."

"That means that he's probably the most influential citizen, as well. He's most likely got that newspaper in his back pocket. You heard my offer. That's my last word."

Gruver left the lounge, stopping on the way out to pay for the meals.

Colfax figured the timing just about right. He had finished one glass of brandy when Gruver walked into the lounge.

"Well, Mr. Colfax," said the cowboy, "it surprised the hell

out of me, but you got a deal. The boss says to bring you on out."

"You explained my terms to him?"

"Just like you said. No guarantees. All you promise is to talk to him."

"You got our train tickets?"

"Well, no, sir. I figured I better ask you first."

"Go get them."

"Uh, which train, Mr. Colfax?"

"The next one west, boy. Time's wasting."

"Yes, sir."

Gruver turned to hurry out of the room. He stopped, hesitated, then turned back to face Colfax.

"Uh . . ."

"I'll be right here."

Chapter Two

Colfax stepped off the train behind Gruver at the depot in Pullman, Colorado, a little town that had first existed for the local ranchers but had grown considerably since the arrival of the railroad. He noticed immediately that the air was crisp and fresh. Although Pullman lay on the flat and dusty plain, Colfax could see the mountains capped in snow off to the west. As he stood taking deep breaths, tasting the air, a burly white-haired man came toward him with long strides. As he got close, the big man's eyes moved from Colfax to Gruver, who was standing close behind and to Colfax's left.

"Boyd," said the big man, "this Colfax?"

"Yes, sir, Mr. Lanagan. This is Mr. Oliver Colfax. Mr. Colfax, my boss, Tiff Lanagan,"

Lanagan stuck a hammy hand out toward Colfax, who gave it a quick squeeze.

"Colfax," said the rancher, "we've got a lot to talk about."

"In the morning, Mr. Lanagan. Right now I want a hotel room, a bath, a good meal, a few drinks, and I want to know about the traveling players."

"All right," said Lanagan. "Follow me. I've got a room waiting for you. The best in town. I don't reckon it can match what you got in Saint Looie, but it ain't bad. Boyd, take care that Mr. Colfax's luggage gets over to the Railhead."

"Yes, sir," said Gruver.

"Come on, Colfax," said Lanagan, and he led the way down the main street of Pullman. The street ran east and west, and Colfax found himself walking alongside Lanagan directly toward the distant mountains. Low-floating cumulus clouds clung to the tops of some of the snowcapped peaks. They walked two blocks down the street and then crossed it to enter the Railhead Hotel, a two-story structure with an ornate facade, clearly the second most impressive building in the town. Down at the far end of the street a more imposing architectural form loomed incongruously over the scene. Inside the lobby of the Railhead, Lanagan issued orders to the desk clerk.

"Monroe," he said, "this is Mr. Oliver Colfax. Give him the key to the suite I reserved for him and have a bath drawn."

"Yes, sir," said the clerk.

"Colfax, this is Monroe Bates. Anything you want, you tell Monroe, and if he don't get it for you, let me know."

"Could I just get you to sign the register, Mr. Colfax?" said Bates.

"Sure thing."

As Colfax was signing the book, Bates snapped his fingers at an underling to get the bath prepared. Lanagan reached into one of his coat pockets and withdrew a ticket, which he held out to Colfax.

"Here's your ticket to that play that's coming to town," he said. "The actors is supposed to be pulling into town either tonight late or sometime in the morning. They're traveling in three wagons, so they can't exactly be precise about their arrival time. I look for them in the morning myself."

"Where's the theater?" asked Colfax.

"You seen it straight ahead of us as we was walking down here. Right at the end of the street. Opry house. I had it built a few years ago for my wife."

"Your bath will be ready in a moment, Mr. Colfax," said Bates, handing him the room key. "Will you be needing anything else?"

"A bottle of Courvoisier," said Colfax, "and Mr. Lanagan's boy, Gruver, is supposed to be bringing my luggage over from the depot."

"I'll have it sent up to your room as soon as it gets here."

Colfax turned to head up for his room, but Lanagan stopped him with his commanding voice.

"When do we talk, Colfax?"

Colfax turned and looked Lanagan in the eyes. The old man had the look, he thought, of one of those old-timers who carved his empire out of Indian country by means of his fists and his guns. A hard man. Colfax mistrusted him. He had the look and the manner of a man who would do anything to hold on to what he fancied belonged to him.

"In the morning," he said, "over breakfast."

"I'll meet you right here at six o'clock," said Lanagan.

"Make it seven," said Colfax. Then he turned and headed for the stairway.

Soon Colfax was up to his chin in hot water. The tub had been placed in the center of the room, and just beside it was a small table with a bottle of Courvoisier brandy and a glass. On the other side of the tub was a straight wooden chair with a stack of fresh towels on it. Before climbing into the tub, Colfax had rolled a cigarette and lit it, then placed an ashtray on the table beside the brandy bottle. He finished the cigarette, snubbed it out, and poured himself a glass of brandy. His luggage had been brought up to the suite within a few minutes after he had climbed the stairs, so there was no reason for him to be disturbed. He had locked the door, and he intended to relax for a while. He thought about Lanagan and the possibility of a job—a good-paying job.

He needed the money. But he couldn't quite bring himself to believe Lanagan and Gruver. These big ranchers had a way of running over anyone who might get in their way, smaller ranchers, sheepmen, farmers, anyone who dared to believe that the open range was actually open, the public domain actually public. If they couldn't buy them off cheap or intimidate them, they would simply label them rustlers and have them killed. Colfax had sworn off work like that. He would not murder for Lanagan or for anyone else.

But there was trouble in the area, and if Colfax or someone didn't do something about it soon, someone would get killed. *Well,* he thought, *that ain't my worry. All I promised Lanagan was a talk. I'll talk to the man, watch* Titus *and get the hell out of this country. Go somewhere. Find something to do.* Then the image of a full-scale range war developing around the small town of Pullman came into his mind, and he thought of Sarge. What would Sarge Luton do in a situation like this? If Sarge were there to advise him, what would Sarge tell him to do? He tossed down his brandy and refilled the glass. Well, he would see Lanagan in the morning.

Following a meal in the hotel restaurant, which he charged to the bill that Lanagan would eventually pay, Colfax strolled out onto the street. He was again surprised by the freshness of the air. He turned west to look at the "opry house" where the performance of *Titus Andronicus* would be held, and he saw three wagons pulled up in front of the imposing edifice. In the lead was an ambulance painted green. Two straight-sided freight wagons followed. The freight wagons were covered in white canvas. All three were pulled by mules. Colfax could see some lettering painted on the sides of the wagons, but he was too far away to read it. As he got closer, he could see a number of men working to unload the wagons, hauling material into the building. Then he got close enough to read the lettering:

ADRIAN CHANNING THEATRICAL COMPANY.

"Hello there," he called as he neared the wagons.

A young man dressed like a cowboy looked up from his work. "Howdy," he said.

"Are you with this company?" asked Colfax.

"Naw, not really. I just happened to be here. They offered me a job helping to unload."

"You have the look of a cowman," said Colfax.

"Work's work," said the young man. "Here comes the man you want to see."

An older man had just stepped out the front door of the opry house, headed back to the wagons for another load. The cowboy heaved another box out of the lead wagon and turned toward the building.

"He's the boss."

Colfax turned his attention to the older man.

"Mr. Channing?"

"Yes, I'm Adrian Channing. And you, sir?"

Colfax held out his right hand, which the older man gripped firmly.

"Oliver Colfax, Mr. Channing. This is a great pleasure for me. I've come from St. Louis, Missouri, to see this production. I never thought to see *Titus Andronicus* played."

"It is a bit unusual, Mr. Colfax, but I thought that it might be appropriate for the far west."

"May I offer you some help?"

"Why, thank you, sir. Grab the other end of this long crate here and help me take it in."

Two more men came out of the building and moved back toward the wagon as Colfax helped Channing pull out the long crate. In about an hour the wagons were unloaded, the mules stabled, and the actors' housing arranged. Colfax invited them and the cowboy to join him in drinks at the Railhead.

"I assume that tomorrow's set aside for getting the stage prepared and for rehearsing," said Colfax to Channing. "I notice that your opening isn't until the day after tomorrow."

"That's correct," said Channing. "Do you have your ticket for opening night?"

"I certainly do," said Colfax. "I have it right here in my pocket. You don't appear to have a sufficient number of actors for the cast of *Titus*. Are you cutting and doubling?"

"We're cutting as little as possible," said the older actor, "and, therefore, doubling as much as possible. Those of us with the major roles are the only ones not doubling. I myself will portray Titus."

"I guessed as much," said Colfax. He poured himself another brandy. "Who is your Aaron? Will he play it in blackface?"

Channing reached for the bottle and refilled his glass.

"Ah, no, Mr. Colfax. We have a genuine black Shakespearean. He also plays Othello when we do that tragedy, and he plays the Prince of Morocco in *The Merchant of Venice*."

"Well, where is he?"

"He got tired of being told that he couldn't join us in hotels, restaurants, and bars as we travel this great nation, so he just quit trying. He's in the ambulance, I expect."

Colfax banged his hand down on the table and stood up.

"Well, by God," he said, "he can drink in here with the rest of us. A Shakespearean actor kept out in the streets? Not if I have anything to say about it."

The young cowboy then stood up.

"I think I can find him," he said. "I'll bring him around."

He tossed off his drink and left the room. Colfax sat back down.

"Mr. Colfax," said Channing, "I appreciate the gesture, but we really don't want to create any problems here."

"There will be none," said Colfax. "You have my guarantee."

He waved at the bartender, who came hurrying over to the table.

"That cowboy that just left here will be coming back soon with a black man," said Colfax. "They are both guests of mine. If you have any problem with that, I suggest you speak to Mr. Bates."

In a few minutes the cowboy returned, accompanied by the actor who would play Aaron the Moor. Colfax stood up and motioned them over to his table. The black man appeared to hesitate. Channing turned to face him and called out.

"It's all right, Dallas," he said. "Join us."

When the two men reached the table, Channing stood up to make introductions.

"Mr. Colfax," he said, "this is Dallas Potter, actor extraordinaire and our Aaron. Dallas, this is Mr. Oliver Colfax."

Colfax extended his hand.

"Mr. Potter," he said, "it's a great pleasure."

Then he turned to the cowboy.

"I never did get your name," he said.

"Rondo Hughes," said the cowboy, "and, uh, I've heard of you."

"Well, then, by God," said Colfax, beginning to feel his brandy, "let's all sit down and drink."

The actors were scattered around the room at several different tables. At a table some distance away from where Colfax sat with Channing, Potter, and Hughes were two actresses, and in a far corner alone Boyd Gruver sat, his face stern, his eyes narrowed and focused on Oliver Colfax. In response to a question put to him by Colfax, Channing was descanting on the special effects involved in the upcoming production.

"The realism," he said, "will amaze you, Mr. Colfax. A warning will be issued at the door, handed out in print with the playbill, that the weak of heart or stomach had best stay away. Our blood has the look and feel of real blood, and we use two gallons of the stuff for one show. You will actually believe that you have seen Lavinia's hands lopped off. Of course, the play must be played this way or not at all. It's without question the goriest of the Bard's tragedies."

Channing paused to finish his drink; then he leaned back in his chair, pulled a large watch from his vest pocket, and checked the time. He tucked the watch back into its pocket and stood up.

"My children," he roared in his best stage voice, "I'm afraid the hour has come. I must call a halt to these festivities. We have a full day of work before us, and we must begin early. To bed. To bed."

As the actors began leaving the bar or tossing down their drinks in preparation to leave, Channing once more offered his large hand to Colfax.

"It's been a great pleasure, sir," he said. "If we don't see you tomorrow, surely you will see us the next day."

When the actors had cleared out, the bar was left with only a few customers, a half-dozen locals, Hughes and Colfax still at the same table, and Gruver still lurking in the far corner. Colfax shot a look at Gruver, who quickly averted his eyes, but Colfax knew that he was being watched. He wondered if Gruver was under orders from Lanagan or had simply assumed the job himself. He turned back to Hughes.

"So you're a cowhand," he said.

"Yeah."

"Out of work?"

"How'd you guess?" said Hughes. "Why, I do odd jobs like unloading them wagons all the time just for my own amusement."

"It must have been a lucky guess. What's the employment situation like around here for cowhands? I'd have thought that there would be plenty of work."

"Your kind of work maybe. Not mine."

Colfax poured himself another brandy, hesitated, glanced at Hughes's empty glass, and held out the bottle.

"Thanks," said Hughes. He took the bottle and poured himself a drink.

"There's a couple of big ranches all right, and then a few smaller ones. There's even a handful of guys like me who come in here thinking they could get a start on a small spread of their own."

"Come in with cows?"

"No."

"How do you get a start from nothing? A little rustling?"

"Mister, I appreciate the drink," said Hughes, "but I don't have to take that kind of talk for it."

"Take it easy, Mr. Hughes," said Colfax. "I'm just asking. Not accusing."

"It's still legal to pick up unbranded strays on open range, mister, even if the big boys don't agree."

"All right. That makes perfect sense to me. I accept your answer. So are you on the lookout for mavericks?"

Hughes tossed down his drink and exhaled loudly.

"I was," he said, "but it's getting too damn dangerous out there. Lanagan and Dierks have decided that all the small ranchers around are rustlers. They've been spreading it around that there's going to be some killing if the 'rustlers' don't pack up and get out. So I decided to get out."

"But you're still here."

Colfax poured another drink for himself and one for Hughes.

"I moved into town. I'm out of the cow business. Been picking up odd jobs around town. I'll save up a little pocket change and hit the trail. Say, don't you know all this anyhow? What are you trying to do—decide whether or not to kill me for a rustler?"

"Why do you ask that?" said Colfax.

"Hell, everyone around here knows that Lanagan brought you to town."

"Mr. Hughes," said Colfax, "I'm going to tell you the whole truth, because I think that I kind of like you. Lanagan sent that sullen fellow over there in the corner all the way to St. Louis to offer me a job. I turned him down until I heard about these players who are in town. I want to see their production in a very bad way, so I made Mr. Lanagan a counteroffer. I said that if he would pay my way out here, I would talk to him about his situation. I made no promise to go to work for him, and I won't go to work for him unless I can satisfy myself that he is in the right. I do not murder for hire."

Rondo Hughes scratched his head.

"Well," he said, "I'll be damned."

"In the morning," Colfax continued, "I'm meeting with Lanagan to hear his side of the story. Then I'll nose around and talk to some other people. But I won't make a decision until I'm convinced of what's right in this situation. Right now I'm going to have to turn in. That appointment I mentioned is early. Where can I find you?"

"Oh," said Hughes, "just around town. I'm sleeping in the stable. Jerry Slayton, he owns it. He lets me stay there in exchange for helping him out a bit."

Colfax stood up and put his hat on.

"Well," he said, "I'll be seeing you, Mr. Rondo Hughes. Good night."

Colfax turned and headed for the door. As he did, he caught a glimpse of Gruver rising from his chair. Outside the door Colfax hurried to the stairs and headed up toward his room. At the top of the stairs he ducked into a dark corner and waited. Gruver came up the stairs and stood looking down the hallway. Colfax slipped the Colt out of its high holster and aimed it at Gruver's back, chest high. He pulled back the hammer. At the click, Gruver turned, startled, reaching for his sidearm. He stopped, his hand on the butt of his six-gun when he saw the barrel of Colfax's Colt aimed directly at him.

"This is twice, boy," said Colfax. "If there's a third time, I'll kill you. What the hell are you following me for anyhow?"

Gruver stammered.

"I'm waiting for an answer," said Colfax.

"I'm just trying to look out for Mr. Lanagan's interests," said Gruver.

"By spying on me?"

"That was one of the rustlers you were drinking with."

Colfax reached out with his left hand and removed the six-gun from Gruver's holster. He tucked it in the waistband of his own trousers.

"That's what I'm here to find out, Gruver," he said. "I'm meeting with Lanagan in the morning. I'll decide who to believe after that. In the meantime I don't work for Lanagan or anyone else, and you stay the hell out of my way."

"What about my gun?"

"Just be glad I don't throw you down the stairs. Now get the hell out of here."

Colfax watched as Gruver descended the stairs and left the hotel. Then he went to his room, locked the door, and fell across the bed.

Chapter Three

It was fifteen minutes past seven when Colfax walked into the room where Lanagan was impatiently waiting. Colfax had been ready, could have met the man on time, but he had delayed purposely. He wanted to test Lanagan's patience. He figured that the cattle baron was used to getting his way, having people leap when he said frog. If he was irritated, he might tend to be less careful about what he said. Colfax didn't want to hear a carefully prepared speech. As Colfax neared the table, Lanagan spoke gruffly to Gruver, who was sitting beside him.

"Get that waiter over here," he ordered.

"Morning, Mr. Lanagan," said Colfax, taking a seat.

"Colfax," said Lanagan, "I'll get right to the point."

"Not yet. I talk business after I eat."

Lanagan's face reddened, but he didn't say anything. Gruver returned, followed by the waiter. Colfax looked directly at Gruver but spoke to Lanagan.

"This has got to be a private meeting," he said.

Lanagan jerked his head at Gruver, indicating that the young man should take his leave. Gruver stood up.

"I'll be around, Mr. Lanagan," he said.

The waiter was standing patiently by with pad and pencil in hand.

"Flapjacks and bacon," said Colfax, "and black coffee, and keep the coffee coming."

"Same thing," said Lanagan.

They sat in tense silence, drinking coffee, waiting for the meal. Colfax rolled a cigarette and smoked it. The silence continued through the meal.

Lanagan's face stayed red, and he ate fast. Colfax made his a leisurely breakfast. Once the plates had been cleared away and the coffee cups once more refilled, Colfax rolled himself another smoke and lit it. He had tested Lanagan's patience about as far as he cared to.

"Mr. Lanagan," he said, "I've read that newspaper story your hired hand carried to St. Louis. What can you tell me that I don't already know?"

"You may have noticed, Colfax," said Lanagan, "that we're in a valley here. It's a river valley. The river runs down out of the mountains and continues to the east of us. I was the first white man in this valley."

Colfax looked across the table at Lanagan from over his cup. Lanagan quickly continued his tale.

"I know what you're thinking," he said, "but don't bother saying it. I never saw no Indians in this valley. Maybe they came in sometimes. I don't know. But if they had been in the habit of using the valley, when they found me here they gave it up. I ain't going to tell you that I fought Indians to keep my ranch, because I never. I never even seen any of them."

Colfax nodded.

"All right," he said.

"Anyhow, I settled on the north side of the river. A few years later Dierks came in. He settled south. We've always got along together. No problems. The town grew up here. Everything was all right, even when the railroad came in."

"I imagine," said Colfax, "that you and this Dierks just about ruled the valley and the town between the two of you. I'm sure everything was all right. From your point of view."

Lanagan's face darkened more, a purplish hue deepening the red that was already there.

"Well, damn it," he said, "it was. I never heard no complaints."

"You wouldn't," said Colfax. Lanagan clenched his teeth but otherwise ignored the comment.

"Until now," he said. "Wheeler came in here about a year ago. He brought a few cows with him, but his herd has increased uncommon fast. He settled in up at the west end of the valley."

"Legal settlement?"

"His settling down there is legal, but rustling ain't."

"Hold on," said Colfax. "You're moving ahead too fast. He running his herd on public land?"

"It's public."

"You and, uh, Dierks run on the public land, too?"

"That's right."

"About that 'uncommon' growth of his herd—picking up mavericks is still legal, isn't it?"

"It's goddamned low, but, yes, it's legal."

Colfax snubbed out his cigarette and then finished off his coffee. He held the empty cup up for the waiter to see.

"Mr. Lanagan," he said, "have you seen any rustling in progress?"

"No, I ain't, but—"

"Have you seen any changed brands?"

"No."

"Why did you send for me? I saw a sheriff's office out there when we walked from the train station. Why doesn't he take care of this?"

"He's like you," said Lanagan. "He keeps asking for proof. Says his hands are tied. If you find the proof, he'll join in and help us clean them out."

The waiter came with the coffeepot, and the conversation abated until he had refilled the cups and gone away again.

"Mr. Lanagan," Colfax continued, "no matter what you've heard about my past, I am not a murderer. I won't kill people for you because you tell me that they're cattle thieves. There are some men around who will do that, and if that's what you want done, you'll have to find one of them."

Lanagan smashed his fist down on the table, causing the recently filled cups to bounce and slosh some of their contents out onto the table. He shouted and stood up out of his chair at the same time.

"Goddamn it, Colfax, I am not a murderer either. I don't want a murderer for hire. I want someone who can stop rustlers. Since Wheeler arrived in this valley, cattle have began to disappear. Not just mine. Dierks's too. We've talked about it. I told you that Wheeler's herd has growed too fast. Then six months ago others come in. Small ranchers, they call themselves. They moved in up behind Wheeler. He brought them in. They're working together. What the hell does it take to convince you?"

"Proof, Lanagan."

"Then go to hell, you son of a bitch. I don't beg nobody. I'll keep my bargain with you. You stay here until you've seen the goddamn play, and I'll pay your bills up until then. Then I'll buy your ticket out of town, and I hope I never see you again."

Lanagan turned abruptly and started to stalk out of the room, but Colfax stopped him.

"Lanagan," he said.

The old man stopped, then turned back toward Colfax, his face a deep purple.

"Lanagan, I'll work for you, but in my own way."

Lanagan stared hard at Colfax from under heavy, furrowed eyebrows.

"Let me investigate and find out for myself if there really is rustling going on here and, if so, who's responsible for it. If I can find that out, get proof, satisfy myself as to where the guilt lies, I'll stop it then."

"Damn it, man, I know it's going on, and I know who's guilty."

"I won't kill anyone just on your say."

Lanagan walked back to the table and sat down again—heavily. He suddenly appeared to be very old and tired, Colfax thought. The cattle baron sat silent for a long moment.

"Hell," he finally said, "that's all I wanted from you in the first place."

"I want to hire me a helper. Will you pay?"

"I got plenty of boys," said Lanagan.

"I don't want one of your boys."

"I'll pay."

"I want a free hand," said Colfax. "I want to be left alone, and I want you to send me in a good horse and saddle."

Lanagan again studied him in silence for a moment. Then he extended his hand across the table. Colfax took it and noted the old man's hard grip.

"We've got a deal," said Lanagan.

They shook hands, and Lanagan turned abruptly and left. The waiter appeared with the coffeepot in hand and looked at Colfax with a sheepish face.

"More coffee, sir?"

"Half a cup," said Colfax. He was still staring after Lanagan. He knew the type. Cattle baron was a good name for them. They were like the medieval barons Colfax knew from the plays of Shakespeare. Rough, uncultured, illiterate or semiliterate, powerful and spoiled bullies, they would trample anything or anyone they found in their way, and nothing would ever convince them they had done anything wrong in the process. In their own eyes they were simply a necessary cog in a necessary social machine. They were fortunate, of course, to have discovered that their cog was the one that drove the entire works.

Yes, Colfax knew the type, and he had been thoroughly prepared to dislike the man. But somehow Colfax sensed an innocence, a naiveté beneath the hard and hoary exterior of Tiff Lanagan. His reaction to the breakfast with Lanagan was beginning to puzzle him. Well, he would give the old man a chance. He would do exactly as he had promised. He would investigate. If he found actual evidence of rustling, he would try to determine who was responsible and stop them. If, on the other hand, his investigation led him to believe that old Lanagan was simply trying to run off smaller ranchers, eliminate his competition, he would leave. He would have no part of that kind of fight. He drained his coffee cup and walked outside just in time to see Lanagan being driven in a buckboard by Gruver on his way out of town. He turned and walked down the street toward the opry house.

The short walk in the crisp morning air felt good to Colfax, and he found himself in a surprisingly chipper mood as he stepped inside the imposing, oversized, ornate front doors of the gaudy monument to Mrs. Lanagan's cultural aspirations. Something about the place was irritating to Colfax. It was superbly constructed and impeccably decorated, but it was—overdone. It was too damn much for this town. In the spot where it stood, it was a bold, declarative statement of bombast and pretentious, tasteless pomposity. As Colfax stood studying the lobby and his own analysis of its builder, one of the doors into the theater proper opened from the inside and Mr. Adrian Channing himself stepped forth.

"Ah, Mr. Colfax," he said, a smile of genuine pleasure spreading across his ruddy face. "How are you this morning?"

He extended his hand, and Colfax took it and gave it a warm shake. This man he liked, this Shakespearean.

"Feeling good, Mr. Channing," he said. "Thank you."

"No ill effects from the festivities of last evening, I presume."

"No. None at all. Is everything here working out all right?"

"Yes, indeed," said Channing. "A beautiful facility, don't you think? By lunchtime we'll have the stage in readiness, and after our repast, we'll rehearse."

"Is there anything I can help you with?"

"Thank you very much, Mr. Colfax, but everything is well under control."

"How about Mr. Potter?" Colfax asked. "Is he being treated well by the local citizenry?"

"As a matter of fact," said Channing, "he's receiving the best treatment he's experienced on this tour, thanks, I believe, to your intercession last night. The word seems to have spread that he has a guardian angel, so to speak, in this town."

"Good. I'll not keep you from your work any longer."

Colfax walked from the theater to the livery stable, where he found a sallow-complected little man at a dusty desk laboring over some figures in a small notebook.

"My name's Colfax," he said.

The gaunt fellow looked up from his arithmetic.

"Jerry Slayton," he said. "I own this place. Heard you was in town. What can I do for you?"

"I'm looking for Mr. Rondo Hughes."

"Oh."

Slayton appeared to be disappointed that he didn't have a customer in Colfax. Then a look of suspicion played across his bony face. He gave Colfax a sideways glance.

"What do you want with him? he said.

"That's my business."

"You going to kill him?"

"I might kill you for being so damned interested in my business."

Slayton rubbed a hand across his face, and Colfax thought that it looked like the thin, brittle skin might tear on the bone beneath it.

"He's out back," said Slayton, "forking hay."

Colfax walked through the stable to the back door and stepped outside again into fresh air.

"Rondo Hughes."

Hughes turned from his work to see who was calling his name.

"Colfax," he said. "What brings you around?"

"Go inside there and tell that whey-faced bastard that you quit," said Colfax. "You're working for me."

Hughes leaned on the handle of the pitchfork and studied Colfax's face for a moment.

"What makes you think I want to work for you?" he said.

"Damn good pay and a hotel room."

"Who do you want me to kill?"

"Maybe no one. Come on."

Hughes tossed the fork to one side and headed for Slayton's office. In less than a minute he was back with Colfax.

"Let's start with the room," he said, "and a bath."

"That's just what I was thinking," said Colfax.

Chapter Four

Colfax and Hughes had their breakfast and walked from the Railhead down the street to Jerry Slayton's stable. It was Colfax's third day in Pullman. Inside the stable they found a grumbling Slayton carrying a bucket of oats.

"I came for my horse," said Hughes.

"You owe me for his keep," said Slayton.

"Put it on Tiff Lanagan's bill," said Colfax. "Did he send a horse and saddle in here for me?"

"Third stall on the right," said Slayton, and he turned his back and started to trudge away.

"Saddle up both animals and bring them out," said Colfax. "Now."

Slayton turned to face Colfax, giving him a hard look. Then he darted his eyes toward Hughes. He looked back at Colfax, dropped his bucket of oats, and went after the horses.

"He's taking it kind of hard," said Hughes, "having to wait on me."

"He's a bad mistake his mother made," said Colfax.

Hughes guffawed.

"So what do we do today, boss?" he asked.

Colfax rolled a cigarette and offered the makings to Hughes, who accepted them and began to roll his own.

"You're going to show me around. I want to see the Lanagan spread, Dierks's and Wheeler's, and those new small ranchers up behind Wheeler. I want to get a feel for the lay of the land."

He took a small tin box out of a vest pocket, flipped open the lid and removed a wooden match. He struck the match on the bottom of the box and held the flame cupped in his hands for Hughes to light his smoke on. Then he lit his own, broke the match, and dropped it and put the box back into his pocket. He took a deep and satisfying draw on the cigarette.

"That sounds easy enough," said Hughes.

"Can we do it and get back to town by seven this evening?"

Hughes expelled smoke from his lungs and looked thoughtful for a moment.

"Yeah," he said. "I think so."

"Good. We're taking in the play tonight."

"Is that part of my job?"

"Anything I tell you to do is part of your job," said Colfax, "until I fire you or you get mad and quit."

Hughes grinned.

"Fair enough," he said.

Jerry Slayton came leading the two saddled mounts out of the stable. One was a roan stallion, a cow pony, the other a larger, black mare, obviously with some Arabian blood. Hughes stepped forward to take the reins of the roan, saving Colfax the trouble of asking which was which. Colfax took the reins of the black from Slayton.

"You paying now?" asked the stableman.

"I told you," said Colfax, "bill Lanagan."

He swung into the saddle, and it felt good to him. He had been too long idling in big-city hotels. He was going to enjoy this day in the saddle. He gave the black a kick in the sides to urge her forward when he heard a thump and a nicker behind him, followed by loud, raucous laughter. He turned to look over his shoulder, hauling back on the reins at the same time. Hughes, still astraddle his saddle, was lying on his side in the dirt, engulfed in a cloud of dust. The roan was fidgeting, and Slayton was slapping his thighs and roaring his enjoyment of his own prank. Colfax turned the black and raced her at Slayton, who took note of his danger too late. He tried to step aside, but the black smashed into him, sideswiping him and catapulting him into a water trough just behind where he stood. Slayton came up out of the water spluttering, spitting, coughing, cursing. As he started to heave himself up out of the trough, he saw the barrel of Colfax's .45 pointed at his face.

"One good joke deserves another, friend," said Colfax.

Hughes looked up from the dirt and laughed.

"Now," said Colfax, "saddle that animal again, and this time do it right."

Slayton did as he had been told, and when he had finished, he sulked against the wall of the stable. Hughes walked over to his horse.

"I think I'll check it this time," he said.

Slayton spat into the dirt.

"I'll get you for this, Rondo," he said.

Hughes, having checked the saddle, climbed into it and swung the roan around to face the surly Slayton.

"Any old time, buddy," he said.

"Mr. Slayton," said Colfax, "I've an idea that the only way you could best Mr. Hughes would be from the back, and if he ever turns up hurt from that particular angle, I'll kill you."

He turned away from Slayton and the stable.

"Which way, Mr. Hughes?" he said.

"Follow me, Mr. Colfax."

Colfax and Hughes had crossed the river early in the day just east of Pullman. They had spent about half the morning studying the lay of Lanagan's spread. Almost everything north of the river, it seemed, was either owned or claimed by Lanagan. The improvements, Colfax noted, were first-rate, and there were plenty of cows out on the prairie. Not as many, of course, as Lanagan thought there should be. Rustlers could get in and drive cattle off in any direction without too much trouble, it appeared, except to the south. To go south they would have to cross the river. But then Lanagan had said that Dierks, on the south side of the river, had also lost cows.

"Mr. Hughes," said Colfax, "is there a decent river crossing anywhere near? Place where a few men could drive cattle across?"

Hughes shoved back his hat and scratched his head.

"Well," he said, "not really. Not unless you ride up into the mountains a ways. There's a place or two up yonder."

"Can we make it that far up today?"

"And get back in time for your playacting?"

"That's my meaning."

"Not to but one of them," said Hughes.

"Then the other'll keep for another time. Show me where Wheeler hangs out."

They were already at the western reaches of the open range that bordered Lanagan's land and then ran into the foothills that quickly steepened into the snowcapped mountain range which cut the valley off from the farther west. Hughes led Colfax along the riverbank on a well-worn trail to a shanty dug into the side of a steep hill. That part of the structure which peeked out of the earth was made of hewn logs and daubed with mud. A thin line of smoke was rising from a stovepipe which jutted forward at an awkward angle just above the topmost log. Colfax had already noted that the temperature had dropped considerably during their short climb.

"This is the place," said Hughes.

"Looks like someone's home," said Colfax. "How many live here with Wheeler?"

"He's got a wife and a couple of younger brothers."

"That's all?"

"Wife's pregnant."

Colfax glanced around. A small corral stood on the downhill

side of the dugout. It was empty. He decided to check his impulse on Hughes.

"Who do you suppose is in that house right now?" he asked.

"I'd say just the missus. The horses are all gone. That means the men are all out riding."

"How far on up to where these other—small ranchers are located?"

"Not far," said Hughes. "That river crossing I told you about? It's just about a mile on up ahead. Just beyond that is where the boys has all dug in. I figure we can ride on up there and look it over, cross on to the other side, then ride back down and get onto Dierks's place."

Colfax bounced his heels against the black mare's sides, urging her forward.

"Let's go," he said.

Just then three riders appeared on the trail above them. They were moving easy, and when they spotted Colfax and Hughes, they halted their mounts. Colfax did likewise. It was a narrow trail. The riders up above eyed Colfax suspiciously. He noticed that one of them had a hand on the butt of his six-gun. All three riders were armed with both six-guns and saddle guns. One rider, the one who appeared to be the oldest, eased his horse forward a few paces. He kept his eyes on Colfax as he spoke.

"Rondo," he said.

"Howdy, Lark," said Hughes.

"What brings you back up to these parts?"

Hughes glanced questioningly at Colfax.

"We got nothing to hide, Mr. Hughes," said Colfax.

"I'm just showing my boss here the lay of the land, Lark."

"And who is your boss?"

"This here is Oliver Colfax, Lark. I'm working for him now. Mr. Colfax, this is Lark Wheeler, and back yonder is Spud and Tommy, his brothers. This is their place we're just passing."

"Colfax, huh?" said Wheeler. "I heard you was working for Tiff Lanagan."

"News travels fast around here," said Colfax. He took note of the fact that the Wheelers' horses were wet up to their flanks, as were the brothers' pantslegs to just below the knees. They had obviously just crossed the river upstream.

"Yeah," said Wheeler. "Bad news. What exactly is it you do for old Lanagan—Colfax?"

"Wheeler," said Colfax, "I'll tell you straight like I'd tell anyone. Lanagan thinks there's rustling going on. I agreed to check into it. If I find it, I'll try to stop it."

"That ain't all of it," said Wheeler. "He told you that it was me doing it, didn't he? And you're up here poking around my place to see what you can see."

Colfax sighed audibly. He pulled the makings out of his pocket and began to roll a cigarette.

"He told me it was you, all right," he said. "You and the others on up the hill. I told him that I wouldn't act on just his say-so. I said I'd look for myself."

Colfax poked the finished cigarette between his lips and fished the tin matchbox out of his vest pocket. He lit the cigarette and replaced the box. There was a long moment of tense silence as Colfax puffed smoke.

"That sounds fair enough," said Wheeler. "Poke around all you want to. We got nothing to hide from you or Tiff Lanagan or anyone else."

"Then maybe you wouldn't mind if I asked you a few questions," said Colfax.

The door to the dugout opened just then, and a young woman stepped out into the cool mountain breeze.

"Lark?" she called. "Lark, dinner's on. We got company?"

Lark Wheeler looked at Colfax a moment before answering.

"Two extra," he called back. Then he glanced at Colfax and Hughes and said in a lower voice, "Put your horses in the corral."

"Mrs. Wheeler, the dinner was excellent," said Colfax, as he pushed back his chair from the table.

"Yes, ma'am," said Hughes. "Thank you kindly."

Mrs. Wheeler blushed slightly as she began clearing the table. She was young. Colfax estimated twenty or twenty-one years at the most. Pretty. Not beautiful but pretty. And she certainly wasn't spoiled. She was likely a good wife for a cattleman, he thought.

"You said you had questions, Colfax," said Wheeler. "Now's your chance."

"All right. Lanagan says your herd has grown too fast. Says it's not natural. Can you explain that growth?"

"Sure. Like everyone else, I pick up mavericks. Hell, even Lanagan and Dierks pick up each other's mavericks. Probably even some of mine. That's part of it. I've also made a couple of runs out since I moved in here and bought a few more head. Lanagan never come around to ask. I could have showed him the bill of sale."

Colfax glanced toward Mrs. Wheeler.

"Do you mind if I smoke in your house, ma'am?" he said.

Mrs. Wheeler blushed once more. Colfax guessed that she was not accustomed to chivalry.

"Why, no," she said. "Not at all."

He rolled a cigarette and offered the makings around the table. Hughes accepted them, as did Lark Wheeler. Spud passed them on, and young Tommy took them. Colfax's eyes rested for a moment on Tommy. Something seemed amiss, but he couldn't quite fasten it down. Tommy rolled himself a cigarette all right, then passed the makings back to Colfax with a grin.

"Thanks," he said.

Colfax passed around the tin matchbox, and while it made the rounds, he spoke again.

"Lanagan believes that you brought in the bunch uphill to help you steal his cattle," he said.

"That son of a bitch," said Spud.

"Shut up, Spud," said Wheeler. "I know some of them boys from back in New Mexico, Colfax. We worked together down there on a couple of big ranches. Rondo here was one of them. I didn't bring them here, though, and we ain't working together."

"Do you have any thoughts on this rustling business?"

"None that I care to voice, Colfax," said Wheeler. He took a deep drag on his smoke. "I mind my own business."

"Have you lost any cattle?"

"No."

Riding up the trail behind Rondo Hughes, Colfax tried to analyze his conversation with Lark Wheeler. Wheeler was sullen but open enough, it seemed. The second brother, Spud, was worse than sullen. He was surly and quick-tempered. Then the young one, Tommy, was—what? Colfax couldn't figure him out. He seemed, well, young. Only Lark Wheeler had done any real talking, and Colfax wondered if he had learned anything at all from Wheeler's talk. Wheeler had invited him to look around. That spoke well for the man. Either he had nothing to hide, as he claimed, or he was awfully confident of his ability to cover his tracks. And of course he had denied all of Lanagan's accusations. He would have done that, guilty or innocent. Two things particularly puzzled Colfax: Wheeler's refusal to offer an opinion on the rustling, and his open admission that he had not suffered any from it. If he was guilty, would he not offer up the opinion that nothing was really going on? If innocent, why not express his opinion? And then his admitting to Colfax that he had lost no cattle had seemed almost like a challenge. Why, if others were losing cattle, had Wheeler not lost any? But if he was guilty and knew that his answer would sound suspicious, why didn't he lie and claim to have lost some like the others?

A shot rang out ahead and startled Colfax out of his thoughts. Hughes's roan whinnied and reared in fright, but Hughes managed to stay in the saddle. He pulled in the reins and fought to get the animal back in control. Colfax halted his black mare and pulled his Winchester out of its saddle boot. He levered a shell into the chamber and searched the hills ahead. Then a shrill voice called out from somewhere up above.

"Rondo Hughes. Rondo. If you brought that killing man

Colfax up here with you, then you both of you just turn right around and ride back on down where you come from."

Chapter Five

"Denny? Denny, that you?" shouted Hughes.

"Get down off your horse, Mr. Hughes," said Colfax. "Now."

Colfax had already dismounted and moved off the trail. Hughes swung his leg over the saddle and stepped down.

"Never you mind, Rondo," came the voice. "You just mount back up and do like I said, or I'll put a hole in you, so help me God I will."

Hughes dropped the reins and stepped up ahead of the roan in the trail.

"Denny," he said, "I know that's you. You ain't going to shoot me. Hell, boy, we ain't after nobody. Just looking around. Talking."

"Who's that with you?"

"Tell him," said Colfax.

"Denny, I've got Oliver Colfax down here with me."

"Just what we figured. You get the hell out of here. I'll drop you both you come any closer."

"Mr. Hughes," said Colfax, "get the hell off the trial."

Hughes hesitated only an instant, then stepped quickly off the trail, pulled his six-gun out of its holster and looked back over his shoulder at Colfax.

"What now, boss?" he said.

"Where is he, Mr. Hughes?"

"Well, I got a pretty good idea. There's a spot up there. We get back out on that trail, he can see us, but we can't see him."

"Can we get around him?"

"Not easy, we can't."

Colfax studied the trail ahead and the surrounding hills. The sound of the river rushing down toward the valley below seemed suddenly almost deafening. *Damn it.* he thought. *Not yet. It's too early. I don't even know what's going on around here. I don't want to kill anyone yet.*

"Rondo?" came the voice, and Colfax was momentarily surprised that the voice could be heard so clearly over the roaring voice of the waters. "Rondo, y'all can't set there all damn day."

He's right, thought Colfax. *I've got things to do elsewhere.*

"Denny," he shouted. "This is Oliver Colfax. Can you hear me?"

There was a slight pause before Denny returned his answer.

"I hear you."

"You come on down here on this trail and talk to us."

"You think I'm crazy?"

"How many men have you killed, Denny?"

Denny was silent, so Colfax continued.

"Well, I've lost count, boy. Now I didn't come up here to kill anyone, but if you don't do like I say, I just might change my mind, and if I decide to kill you, Denny, you're as good as dead."

"What do you want?"

"I just want to ride up on to the crossing and over to the other side. Then I'm going back down again. That's all."

"Well," said Denny, his voice this time barely audible to Hughes and Colfax, "I guess there ain't no harm in that."

"I'm waiting, Denny," called Colfax.

"Okay. I'm coming on down. To talk. Okay?"

Colfax smirked inwardly. It was sometimes handy to have possession of a reputation for notoriety such as his. Sometimes. He could hear Denny scrambling down from behind some rocks. Soon he saw the man, rifle in hand, appear on the trail. Colfax, holding his own Winchester in his right hand, stepped out in view. Denny stood still, staring in awe at the famous killer there before him.

"Mr. Hughes," said Colfax, his voice low and calm, his eyes on Denny, "would you step out here and make the introductions?"

Hughes stepped to the edge of the trail so he wouldn't be directly between Colfax and Denny. He still held his six-gun in his right hand, but his hand was hanging down at his side. He looked from Colfax to the other man.

"Mr. Colfax," he said, "this is a—uh—a friend of mine, Denny Doyle. Denny, this is Mr. Oliver Colfax here."

"How do you do, Mr. Doyle?" said Colfax.

Denny Doyle shifted his weight nervously from one foot to the other while looking mostly at the ground.

"Howdy," he said.

"Mr. Doyle," said Colfax, "are Mr. Hughes and I trespassing on your private property?"

"Huh? Well, no?"

"Then why did you fire on us?"

"I never meant to hit nobody. Hell, Colfax, I'm a pretty damn good shot."

"That's true," said Hughes. "If he'd a wanted to drop me, he'd a done it."

"All right," said Colfax, "then why were you trying to run us off of this public road?"

"Well," said Doyle, "I was kind of—elected. The boys said for me to do it."

"The boys?"

"Yeah. The other—ranchers up here with me."

"May I ask why?"

Doyle looked from Colfax to Hughes, then back down at the dirt between his boots. He was young. Colfax judged him to be in his mid-twenties, about the same age as Hughes. And he had the look of a cowboy, all right, though one who had seen some hard times. Colfax would hardly have graced the man with the term "rancher."

"Well, damn it, Colfax," said Doyle, "they said that Tiff Lanagan had hired you to come up here and wipe us out. We're just defending ourselves."

It's the same old tune, thought Colfax, *but then, I guess I can't really blame them. Not after the life I've led. Time was they'd have been right. If a man hired Oliver Colfax, someone was going to die.* He let out an audible sigh.

"Mr. Doyle," he said, "Mr. Hughes and I did not come up here shooting nor intending to shoot, and even when you fired on us, we did not shoot back. Now do you suppose we could all ride on up to the crossing together? I'd like to meet your friends—the other ranchers."

"Yeah," said Doyle, "well, I guess so."

The ride up to the crossing was short, as Hughes had said it would be, and soon Colfax found himself in the midst of a hastily constructed community of dugouts, lean-tos, a couple of tents, and brush and log corrals. The structures were scattered seemingly at random on both sides of the river, but on the north side, waiting by the side of the trail upon which Colfax and Hughes rode with Doyle, five armed cowboys stood waiting, their faces and postures belligerent. The three riders halted their mounts within ten feet of the waiting cowboys, but Doyle quickly dismounted and moved with his horse over to the other side. For a long, tense moment, no one spoke. Then the silence was relieved by the man standing in the center of the group of cowboys. He was looking at Colfax as he spoke to Doyle.

"Denny," he said, "we told you to turn them back or kill them."

"I know, Youngblood," said Doyle, "but, well, they said they didn't come up here to fight. Colfax there, he said he wanted to meet you."

"I bet he did," said Youngblood. "Colfax, you murdering son of a bitch, you just rode into your death trap."

"Hold on," said Hughes. "Y'all don't need to go killing anyone."

Youngblood turned his gaze on Hughes for the first time.

"I'm surprised at you, Rondo," he said, "riding with someone like that. You should've stayed up here with us."

"Or in the stable," said Denny Doyle.

"Well," said the cowboy standing to Youngblood's immediate left, "we going to kill them?"

Colfax decided that he had let this potentially volatile conversation go unchecked long enough.

"Mr. Youngblood," he said, "you seem to be in control here. There are six of you over there and two of us. You can kill us if that's what you're determined to do. Now I'm not sure of Mr. Hughes's abilities, but I know that I can kill two of you, maybe three, before I go down. You've obviously heard of me, so you know I'm not lying. And you, Mr. Youngblood, will be the first I drop. So what's it going to be?"

"He said he just wanted to talk to us," said Doyle, a nervous tremble in his voice.

"So talk," said Youngblood.

"I'm investigating rustling for Tiff Lanagan," said Colfax. "I've looked over the Lanagan spread, stopped to talk with the Wheelers, now you. I'm going on down to meet Dierks next, unless you stop me here."

Colfax paused, but it was apparent to him soon that neither Youngblood nor any of his cohorts intended to say anything, so he continued.

"I don't know anything," he said. "I'm looking, and I'm asking."

"Asking what?" said Youngblood.

"Do you believe that there are rustlers operating around here?"

"Hell, no. That's Lanagan's excuse to try to run us out of here. He wants it all for himself. Don't want no competition. There ain't no rustlers around here."

"Did you bring cows in here with you when you came?"

"A few. Mostly we picked up mavericks."

"Where do you keep your herd?"

Youngblood glanced around his group of surly cowhands and shot a quick look in Hughes's direction before he answered.

"We run them down on the prairie, open range, same as Wheeler, same as Dierks, same as old Lanagan himself."

"I didn't see anything down there today that didn't have the Lanagan brand on it," said Colfax.

"We just sold everything we had," said Youngblood. "Ain't got a cow amongst us just now."

"So what do you do next?" asked Colfax.

"Look for mavericks again. You got any more questions?"

"I guess not," said Colfax. "Not just now."

"Then why don't you and old Rondo just cross on over, if that's what you want to do, and ride back down the hill?"

"I believe we will, Mr. Youngblood," said Colfax, touching the brim of his hat. "Thank you."

Colfax realized, as he rode behind Rondo Hughes on the way back down, that it was easy enough to believe that Youngblood and his ragtag bunch of ill-tempered ruffians were a gang of rustlers. He would have to be careful not to jump to conclusions, not to read circumstantial evidence or too little evidence as conclusive. His intuition told him that the Wheelers were straight. Lark was anyway, and Lark controlled his brothers, the surly Spud and the—and Tommy. But that bunch on up the hill were another story.

"Mr. Hughes," he called.

Hughes twisted in the saddle to look back at Colfax.

"Yeah?"

"Do you think that bunch back there is guilty of rustling?"

The trail was wide enough, so Hughes held back his roan to allow Colfax to ride up beside him.

"We don't even know yet that there's been any rustling, do we? Ain't that what you been saying?"

"Yeah," said Colfax. "I did say that, but you know those men. You used to stay up there with them. I asked you what you think."

"Aw, I don't know them all that well," said Hughes. "I threw in with them down in New Mexico. Youngblood said this would be a good place to get a start. He'd been up here before, I guess. I rode along. We all picked up mavericks. Wasn't nobody rustling, though. Not while I was there. Not that I seen."

"Why did you decide to pull up stakes?" asked Colfax.

"The pickings was too slim, and then Lanagan started his bellyaching. I thought I'd get out before it got too dangerous."

"And now here you are back in the middle of it," said Colfax.

"But the pay's a lot better, boss. A whole lot better."

Dierks was a real surprise to Colfax. A short, slight man with an eastern dialect, he was balding and wore a neatly trimmed mustache. He was dressed in a suit and tie, but had pulled off the jacket, leaving the vest on and buttoned.

What was I expecting? Colfax asked himself. *Another Lanagan, I guess.* Dierks had been polite and precise. He was pleased to meet Mr. Colfax, relieved to know that Colfax would be looking into the situation. Yes, he had lost cattle. Did he know who was responsible? No, not really. Mr. Lanagan was positive that it was Wheeler and those others up there, but Dierks really didn't know. Would Mr. Colfax be at the play this evening, he wondered.

"Yes, indeed," said Colfax. "I will certainly be there."

"Oh, good," said Dierks. "Then I shall probably see you there."

There was no one, thought Colfax, sitting in his bath, no one but Youngblood and his bunch. It had to be them. Youngblood had said that he grazed his cattle down on the prairie on the public domain, but Colfax had seen plenty of evidence of cattle on the riverside trail, and the evidence continued well beyond Wheeler's outfit, on up and seemingly beyond Youngblood's ratty cow camp. Well, he had his suspects, but he realized that he had reached this point in precisely the same manner as Lanagan had reached his. The only difference was that Lanagan included the Wheelers in with the suspected rustlers. What Colfax needed now, more than ever, was proof of rustling, then proof that Youngblood and company was guilty. Tomorrow he would go to work on that. Tonight was the play.

Chapter Six

The performance was magnificent. It exceeded Colfax's hopes and expectations. It was more than he imagined it would be, from the moment Samuel Chase as Saturninus stepped on the stage and began the brief expository opening scene.

Nobel patricians, patrons of my right,
Defend the justice of my cause with arms;
And, countrymen, my loving followers,
Plead my successive title with your swords.

The emperor of Rome had just died, and Saturninus was wanting to be declared his heir, but his younger brother, Bassianus, was challenging his right. In the midst of the quarrel, Titus Andronicus, a powerful and respected Roman general, returned to Rome from the Gothic wars, bringing with him prisoners, including Tamora, the Queen of the Goths, and three of her sons. Soon Titus allowed his sons to brutally execute one of Tamora's sons out of revenge for the death in battle of a brother of theirs, leaving alive of the queen's sons only Chiron and Demetrius. Titus, played with impressive bombast by Mr. Adrian Channing, gave his political support to Saturninus, thereby helping him to the throne. In gratitude, the new emperor decided to marry Titus's daughter, Lavinia, played to perfection thought Colfax, by Mrs. Alma Dyer. But Lavinia was already betrothed to Bassianus, and the two lovers ran away. Emperor Saturninus blamed Titus, and he took for his new wife and empress the prisoner Queen of the Goths, Tamora.

Tamora, played by Mrs. Dixon Lindsay, planned to use her new position of power to avenge herself on Titus for her defeat in battle, her capture, and the death of her son. All this, Colfax thought, was accomplished cleanly and clearly and in a short time. In spite of the complexities of the plot, Mr. Channing's company played it so well that anyone not drunk or asleep or hopelessly thick-skulled should have been able to keep up with the characters and their desperate situations.

Then when Mrs. Lindsay as Tamora spoke her first aside to Saturninus revealing her secret intentions, Colfax felt a thrill rush through him.

My lord, be ruled by me, be won at last;
Dissemble all your griefs and discontents:
You are but newly planted in your throne.
Lest then the people, and patricians too,
Upon a just survey, take Titus' part,
And so supplant you for ingratitude,
Which Rome reputes to be a heinous sin,
Yield at entreats, and then let me alone.
I'll find a day to massacre them all,
And raze their faction and their family,
The cruel father, and his traitorous sons
To whom I suéd for my dear son's life;
And make them know what't is to let a queen
Kneel in the streets, and beg for grace in vain.

But it was Act Two that Colfax was particularly anxious to see. It began with the entrance and soliloquy of Aaron, the Moor, played by Mr. Dallas Potter, who was in the service of Tamora and was her secret lover. Mr. Potter was an especially evil Aaron and a surprisingly satisfying speaker of Shakespeare's lines. Things happen fast in *Titus Andronicus*. No sooner was Aaron introduced than he discovered that Tamora's two sons, Chiron and Demetrius, played, quite capably Colfax thought, by Mr. Woodward Granger and Mr. Tyndall Tabor, were lusting after Lavinia. A hunt was organized, and out in the woods, Bassianus and Lavinia came across Tamora and her two sons. Aaron had already instructed the sons what to do to satisfy their lust. Tamora watched as the two stabbed Bassianus and held Lavinia captive. They made clear their plans to rape her, then dragged her screaming off the stage along with the body of her husband. Colfax noticed the audience grow nervous at this scene, but two women fainted and several left the theater when Lavinia returned, blood streaming from her mouth and from two stumps where her hands had been. While the lovely young woman bled horribly, the two brothers gleefully recounted to each other how they had raped her, then cut out her tongue and cut off her hands. Channing had been right, Colfax thought. The effect was realistic, too realistic, obviously, for some members of the audience.

Those who managed to stay through the bloody entrance of Lavinia held out for the rest: the onstage lopping off of Titus's hand with blood shooting in spurts clear past the apron of the stage and into the orchestra pit, accompanied by a ghastly shriek from deep in the lungs of Adrian Channing; the carrying onstage of the heads of Titus's sons, looking exactly like the heads of the two actors who played the parts, also dripping blood; Titus's slicing the throats of Chiron and Demetrius and filling a basin with their blood as it ran from the fresh wounds; the final horror when Titus stabbed his own daughter, Lavinia, to death, stabbed Tamora, and was himself stabbed to death by Saturninus, who was then stabbed by Titus's remaining son, Lucius. All of these killings were accompanied by the Channing company with liberal use of the theatrical blood which had characterized the entire production. *He said two quarts,* thought Colfax. *It seems much more.*

Not everyone in Pullman who attended the play was pleased at the performance, but all were impressed by it. Hughes and Colfax had been seated together in a box with a commanding view of both the stage and the house below. Colfax had taken advantage of his position before the opening of the first scene to look over the audience. He had seen Lanagan down there along with Mrs. Lanagan. Dierks was present as he had said he would be. None of that was surprising, but the others were. There was Boyd Gruver, all three Wheeler brothers and Mrs. Lark Wheeler, and Youngblood and two of his punchers. On second thought, though, Colfax realized that he shouldn't have been surprised to see anyone in the theater that night. It had nothing to do with Shakespeare. It was simply something different for people to do. Probably the same people would have been in attendance had the play been by Colley Cibber or Dion Boucicault or had it been a show of dancing girls. When the final applause died down and the curtain calls ceased, Colfax turned to Hughes.

"Well, Mr. Hughes," he said, "what do you think?"

"I don't know what the hell it was all about," said Hughes, "but it sure was a bloody son of a bitch."

"Come on," said Colfax, and he led the way down to the lobby, where he noticed the Wheelers making their way through the crowd toward the big front doors. An ashen-faced Tommy was in the rear, trying to keep up with the rest of his family. *Poor young fellow probably never saw anything like that before in his life,* thought Colfax.

"Ah, Mr. Colfax."

Colfax turned to see Dierks behind him. They shook hands and chatted briefly about the play. Dierks, it seemed, had a genuine appreciation for Shakespeare.

"I do think they could have made a better selection of play, though," said Dierks. "I'm afraid that the gore in *Titus* overpowers the poetry."

"You're probably right about that, Mr. Dierks," said Colfax. "It's a common criticism of the play. On the other hand, I was pleased with the opportunity to see a production of it. I never thought to have the chance."

"Well, I suppose that's one way of looking at it," said Dierks. Just then Tiff Lanagan walked up, his wife a little behind him.

"Hello, Dierks," he said. "Colfax, this is Mrs. Lanagan. Oliver Colfax, my dear.

"It's a pleasure, Mrs. Lanagan," said Colfax. "I've arranged a little reception for the players in the Railhead. Mr. and Mrs. Lanagan, Mr. Dierks, you are all invited to attend."

"Is this going on my bill?" said Lanagan.

"No, Mr. Lanagan, it is not. I wouldn't allow anyone else to pay for this. It's my privilege."

"Then we'll be there. Come along, Agnes."

Colfax, Hughes, Dierks, and the Lanagans had each already had a couple of drinks apiece by the time the players began to arrive. Woodward Granger, Tyndall Tabor, and Alma Dyer were the first to appear.

"I'm afraid that I found both of you gentlemen to be totally repulsive," said Agnes Lanagan.

"Thank you very much," said Granger. "That was, of course, the idea."

"They are rather repulsive," said Alma Dyer, obviously teasing the two actors. "Typecasting, you know."

"Oh, Alma," said Tabor. "Please."

Alma Dyer laughed, a lovely laugh, thought Colfax, like music.

"Mrs. Dyer," he said, "may I congratulate you on a remarkably beautiful performance of an extremely difficult role."

"Why, thank you, Mr. Colfax. And I understand that we also have you to thank for this lovely reception."

"It's my pleasure, ma'am."

Just then Adrian Channing made his entrance, accompanied by Mrs. Dixon Lindsay.

"A roaring success," he shouted.

Colfax moved quickly to see that Channing and Mrs. Lindsay were served.

"Mrs. Lindsay," he said, "you were at once beautifully seductive and appallingly evil, a compelling combination. I congratulate you on a fine performance."

"Thank you, Mr. Colfax. Tamora is a delightfully wicked role."

"And you, Mr. Channing," said Colfax, "are to be doubly congratulated—once for your superb portrayal of Titus, and again for being the mastermind behind this entire effort."

Samuel Chase came into the room, followed almost immediately by C. C. Carpenter, the actor who had played Bassianus. The others, those who doubled and served as extras, had all arrived. Colfax looked around. One person was missing.

"Where is Mr. Potter?" he asked.

"Oh," said Channing, glancing around the room, "I'm sure he'll be along shortly."

Soon the party grew loud and lively. The Lanagans approached Colfax.

"We'll be going home, Colfax," said Lanagan. "I want to talk to you tomorrow."

"I'll stop out," said Colfax.

"A lovely reception, Mr. Colfax," said Agnes Lanagan. "Thank you for inviting us."

The Lanagans left, and the party continued, but Colfax was uneasy. He excused himself to Channing, instructed Hughes to remain as host, and left the Railhead. He was soon at the theater but found it dark and deserted. He checked Channing's wagons, remembering that Channing had said that Potter sometimes slept in the ambulance. The wagons were also deserted. He went by the sheriff's office. It was locked. Back at the party he pulled aside Channing, Dierks, and Hughes.

"Mr. Potter is nowhere to be found," he said.

"What do you mean?" asked Channing.

"I checked the theater and your wagons. Everything appears to be deserted."

"Perhaps Dallas is sleeping in his dressing room," said the old actor.

"Well, let's find out," said Colfax. "Mr. Dierks, are you bold enough to find the sheriff and bring him along to the theater?"

"Yes. I'll get him if I have to drag him out of his bed."

Dierks left immediately, and Colfax continued speaking to the remaining two.

"Mr. Hughes," he said, "check around town. It's unlikely that Mr. Potter would venture out on his own, but check anyway. Mr. Channing and I will be at the theater."

"Okay, boss."

Channing opened up the building with the keys that had been entrusted to him for the duration of his stay in Pullman and began lighting lamps in the lobby. He took one lamp in hand and led Colfax through the lobby and the house and up onto the stage, then backstage to the hallway leading to the dressing rooms. Moving down the hallway in the semidarkness, Colfax stepped in something wet and slick and nearly lost his footing.

"Mr. Channing," he said, "bring your light here."

Channing moved toward Colfax.

"Is that some of your stage blood on the floor?"

"We clean all that up after each performance, Mr. Colfax."

The old man's voice trembled as he lowered the lamp, and Colfax bent over to dip his fingers into the suspicious substance.

"This is blood, Mr. Channing," said Colfax. "Real blood. Go back to the front door and watch for the sheriff."

Channing started to speak, stammered, then handed his lamp to Colfax and started to make his way back through the building. The portions they had gone through on the way were already lit and Colfax followed the trail of blood to a dressing room. On the door a sign bore the name "Mr. Dallas Potter." He went inside and found the room splattered with blood. Real blood. He lit the lamp in the room and went back into the hallway, lighting the lamps there. The trail of blood led to a back door and outside into the darkness.

Chapter Seven

Colfax tried to sleep, but he tossed fitfully in the bed. He had drunk too much liquor at the reception, and then he had discovered the body of Dallas Potter out behind the theater. Someone had apparently surprised Potter in the dressing room after everyone else had left the theater, hacked and stabbed him repeatedly, then sliced his throat from ear to ear, nearly severing the head from the body. Then the murderer had apparently dragged the body out into the hallway, down the hallway to the back door and outside. Colfax was a hard man, a one-time hired killer, and bloodshed and death were things with which he was too familiar. But he had admired Dallas Potter, a black man who must have overcome tremendous odds to become a successful Shakespearean actor. Colfax had not really gotten to know Potter, but he had wanted to. He would have liked Potter. He knew that. Damn whoever had robbed him of that opportunity. He wanted to find the murderer and make him pay for his deed.

Then there was the other business. He had committed himself to a job, and Colfax had always fulfilled his commitments. It was a matter of pride and honor. He had not really wanted this job, had taken it only as a convenient way of getting to Pullman to see the performance of *Titus Andronicus*, and his heart was not really in the hunt on this one. Yet he had committed himself to it, so he had to try to find evidence of rustling and then stop the rustlers, if indeed there were any. He was almost certain that Youngblood and the other down-and-out cowhands Rondo Hughes had abandoned were the guilty ones. But how to prove it? He remembered that he had promised Lanagan he would stop by for a talk. Damn it. He wanted to pursue the trail of the murderer of Potter, but he had promised. He'd have to go out to Lanagan's ranch and give him a report. He guessed that it wouldn't take too long. He'd go early and get it over with, then get back to town and begin to investigate the murder. But where would he start? Tracks? Tracks. He'd have to go back to the theater at first light. Lanagan would have to wait a little. He couldn't take a chance that tracks, or any other kind of evidence there might be, might be wiped out before he'd seen them, and he didn't trust that fool sheriff, Dort, to do anything right.

Colfax rolled over onto his stomach. The sheet was sticking to his sweaty flesh, and when he rolled, he wrapped himself in it. He turned back again onto his back trying to unwrap himself, but the tangle only seemed to get worse. He realized that he was beginning to think like a lawman. He had two cases to work on at the same time. He would be searching for evidence and trying to track down the guilty in both cases at the same time. Why? It had just happened, he supposed. In the case of the rustling business, it was a matter of honor. He had taken a job. He had given his word. In the murder case, he cared. He was mad. But wasn't it ironic? Colfax acting and thinking like a lawman. He wondered what Sarge would have thought had he known about it. He would like to see Sarge.

Hell. Obviously he couldn't sleep. He ripped at the wet sheet, finally freeing himself, and stood up naked in his room. He found the lamp and lit it, turning the flame low. Then he got his makings and rolled himself a cigarette. He lit the cigarette and took a deep drag. He wished that he knew who it was he was after, so he could just go out and find them and kill them and get it over with. He was getting too old for all this, he realized. He should find another way to make a living. Once these two cases were disposed of, he thought, he would call it quits. Yes. It was just about quitting time. He was tired.

Colfax was at the theater before the sun was quite up. Hardly anyone in Pullman was yet stirring. He had noticed on his way that the sheriff's office was still closed. The opry house was locked when he arrived at it, and he cursed softly, then admitted to himself that he should have expected that. He walked around to the back where he had discovered the body. The ground was dry and dusty, but Colfax could see the tracks of a horse. He studied the bloodstains, which were still sticky, and the marks made where the body had been dragged. It appeared to him that a man had dragged the body out the back door, left it there in the dirt, then mounted a waiting horse and ridden away—to the west. Colfax studied the hoofprints long and hard, trying to memorize them, hoping that if he ever saw prints made by the same horse again, he'd know them. Even as he studied, though, he knew that it was futile. They were not that clear, and, as far as he could tell, there was nothing particularly distinctive about them. The footprints of the man, the murderer, were no clearer. They were boot prints, cowboy's boots. That was about all he could tell.

He stood up and ran his hand through his hair. He hated to waste the time, but he knew that he needed some food before he started on what he knew would be a long, tough day. Some food and some coffee. Lots of coffee after the short and restless night he had spent. He walked back to the Railhead, and went into the cafe, and ordered a breakfast.

"Keep the coffee coming," he told the waiter.

Colfax had finished his breakfast and was drinking a last cup of coffee when Rondo Hughes walked in and sat down at the table.

"Morning, boss," said Hughes.

"Morning. I've finished eating, but you can go ahead and order."

"No thanks," said Hughes. "I've done et down the street. It's cheaper, and some friends of mine hang out there."

"Good," said Colfax. "We've got a busy day ahead of us. I've got to go out and see Lanagan. I'll give him a quick report of what we did yesterday to content him for the time being. Then I'm coming back to town to see what I can determine about that— killing last night."

"That was a bad business," said Hughes. "What do you make of it?"

"I don't know."

"Well, I'd say you'll find plenty of suspects. Just look for folks who don't like uppity niggers."

Colfax took a last sip from his coffee cup, put the cup down on the table, and looked at Hughes.

"Does that include you, Mr. Hughes?" he asked.

"Well," said Hughes, "I ain't going to tell you that I was happy to be sitting at the same table with him the other night, but I don't kill folks over a thing like that."

"That's my worry, anyhow," said Colfax. "I want you to ride back up that trail we took yesterday. There were cattle tracks going up beyond Youngblood's hangout. I want to know where they go. If there's a way for you to get up there without being seen, take it. Look for cattle up there, or evidence of where they've been. See me back here later."

"It'll take a little longer to get there," said Hughes, "but there's another trail north a piece. I think I can get up there without anybody knowing it."

"Mr. Lanagan," said Colfax, "there have been cattle up that trail past Wheeler's place and on beyond where Youngblood and that other bunch are camped out. It wasn't convenient for me yesterday to go up the trail and follow the tracks, but I've got a man on that right now."

"I knew it," said Lanagan. "Wheeler and Youngblood. I knew it."

"Just hold on a minute. I said I had seen tracks. I don't yet have any hard evidence of rustling. I'm still investigating. At this point, I have a tendency to halfway agree with you. I don't think that Wheeler and the others are working together, and I don't think that Wheeler and his brothers are rustlers. I do think that our likely suspects are Youngblood and his bunch. At least that's where I'm going to look first."

The door opened and Agnes Lanagan came into the room carrying a silver tray containing two cups and other implements.

"Coffee, Mr. Colfax?" she said.

Colfax stood up.

"Thank you, Mrs. Lanagan," he said. "Yes, I will."

Colfax took a cup off the tray and sat back down as Agnes Lanagan turned to offer the other cup to her husband.

"I'll leave you gentlemen to discuss business," she said, and she left the room.

"Agnes is a fine woman," said Lanagan.

"Yes, indeed," said Colfax. "You're a fortunate man."

"Yeah. Colfax, I need to have this rustling business cleaned up quick.

"It's not just that I'm losing money. That's bad enough, but there's more to it than that. I'm afraid of a war. I don't want that to happen in this valley. My men are getting restless. They want to ride up that mountain and start shooting. Dierks is having the same problem, and there are people in town who aren't even directly involved who are talking the same way. So far it's just talk, but I don't know how long I can keep it that way."

Colfax sipped at the dainty cup in which Agnes Lanagan had served him coffee. He didn't like the cup. It made him nervous. He was afraid that he would drop it. In fact, Agnes Lanagan's house made him feel that same way. He wasn't sure that he should have stepped on her carpets. He was worried that his bulk might somehow rumple the chair he sat on. The cup rattled against its saucer when Colfax put it back down.

"Mr. Lanagan," he said, "I'll do everything I can to hurry this business along. I promise you that."

He stood up and a bit awkwardly placed the cup and saucer on a small table which stood beside the chair.

"Please give Mrs. Lanagan my thanks for her hospitality," he said. "I have work to do."

As Colfax stepped off the Lanagan porch, Boyd Gruver rode up. Gruver stayed in his saddle and looked down at Colfax.

"Howdy, Colfax," he said.

Colfax touched the brim of his hat and nodded.

"Gruver," he said.

"I take it you're still working for Mr. Lanagan."

"That's right."

"You making any progress?"

"Boy," said Colfax, "that's between me and your boss."

Rondo Hughes rode easy in the saddle. He had taken the same route as the one he had led Colfax over the day before, along the river on the north side up to the foothills that led into the mountains. From there the trail wound past the Wheelers' cabin and on up to the camp of Youngblood and his bunch. He allowed his roan to move at a leisurely pace as he began the climb. Hughes didn't seem to be particularly anxious or alert. He was certainly in no hurry. As he passed by the Wheeler cabin, he waved at Mrs. Wheeler, who was out in the yard washing. He continued on up the trail. Even when he reached the spot on the trail where Denny Doyle had fired on him the day before, Hughes did not glance up, did not look around, did not slow his pace. He continued along the trail. He wound his way around the sharp curve and rode underneath the very rock behind which Doyle had hidden. Soon he would be at Youngblood's camp.

"Hello, Rondo."

Hughes pulled back lightly on the reins and halted the roan in the middle of the trail. The voice had come from behind him. He turned slowly and looked over his shoulder, a smile on his face.

There standing behind him in the trail, an 1860 model Henry .44 rifle cradled in his arms, was Youngblood.

"Howdy, Youngblood," said Hughes.

Youngblood shifted his weight from one leg to the other and let his right hand, holding the Henry, drop to his side.

"Rondo," he said, "I sure didn't expect to see you back up here so soon."

Chapter Eight

"Go ahead, Mr. Channing," said Sheriff Dort. "Open her up."

Adrian Channing unlocked the front door of the theater building and stepped aside to allow Dort to enter first. Colfax went in behind Dort, and Channing followed, closing the door after himself. The three men walked through the lobby of the house, climbed up onto the stage, and made their way backstage to the hallway which ran past the dressing rooms. The bloodstains were still there. Dort pointed to a smear on the floor.

"What the hell's that?" he said.

"That's where I slipped last night," said Colfax.

"Oh."

"But here's something a little more interesting."

Colfax knelt to get a closer look. There were boot prints in the blood, and they were much more distinct than those he had found outside in the dirt. The murderer was apparently careless in the dark hallway while dragging the body. He had stepped in the blood and left clear tracks. The boot was small. Colfax guessed a size seven or so, but even more telling was the fact that the print of the right boot showed a clear gash across the sole. These prints would be easily spotted anywhere else they might be found. Of course, the killer likely had discovered his bloodstained boots and discarded them by this time. Still, it was a definite clue.

"Who'd ever thought a nigger to have so much blood in him," said Dort.

"No more than you,"said Colfax. Damn, he thought. Hughes was right.

Trying to track this murderer in the community could lead up several dozen trails. He had a feeling that Dort was not going to be an enthusiastic investigator. He stood up and moved to the dressing-room door, opened it, and stepped inside. Several minutes of searching turned up nothing of any apparent help. The boot print revealing the slashed sole remained the only item of value gained from the search of the building.

"Thank you, Mr. Dort," said Colfax. "Mr. Channing."

"Colfax,"said Dort.

Colfax had already turned to leave. He stopped and faced the sheriff.

"Yes?"

"You're conducting your own private investigation of this here killing. I don't know what your reasons are for doing that, but if you come up with anything, you keep me informed. You hear?"

Colfax looked at Dort for a moment, then gave him a short nod.

"Mr. Colfax," said Channing, "would you have a drink with me?"

Channing looked haggard and worn. He looked, Colfax thought, much older than he had seemed just the day before. At his age a theatrical tour such as he had undertaken was bound to be a strain, even without the grisly murder of a member of his company. Colfax put a hand on the old man's shoulder.

"I'll join you," he said.

They sat at a table in the Railhead, Channing with a large glass of whiskey before him, Colfax with coffee. He had decided to cut out the drinking. At least, he thought, until this business was over and done. He needed to keep a clear head.

"I don't know what to do, Mr. Colfax," said Channing. "I don't know if I can develop another Aaron out of my cast. I don't know if the tour can continue."

"I can't advise you," said Colfax. "Why don't you take a couple of days to consider the problem? Discuss it with your company."

Channing swallowed a gulp of whiskey, then was convulsed with a sudden, choking sob. He covered his face with both hands and gave way to uncontrolled weeping. Colfax was uncomfortable. He took out the makings and rolled himself a cigarette, and as he was lighting it, Channing, with a deep breath, regained control of himself.

"I'm sorry, Mr. Colfax," he said. He pulled a wrinkled and soiled handkerchief out of a pocket and wiped his eyes; then he blew his nose into it.

"It's all right, Mr. Channing," said Colfax. "I understand. I'm even a bit envious of your ability to achieve that kind of release."

"But why?" said Channing, his eyes as well as his voice pleading with Colfax for an explanation. "Why poor Dallas? He was such a gentle man. He never hurt anyone in his life."

Colfax took a long drag on his cigarette. He had an answer to Channing's question—perhaps *the* answer, but he didn't want to give voice to it.

"I don't know, sir," he said. "Who can explain human activities?"

"There are more things in heaven and earth, Horatio," said Channing, "than are dreamt of in your philosophy."

"Exactly."

The old man turned up his glass and emptied it, then stood up.

"Well," he said, "I should be getting back to my charges. Thank you, sir, for your company, and for your kindness."

Colfax gestured to the waiter for more coffee as he watched Channing take his leave of the Railhead. *For my kindness,* he thought. *It was my kindness that got Dallas Potter killed.* The idea had begun to form in Colfax's mind that Potter would probably still be alive if he had held to his practice of keeping to himself, but Colfax had enticed him into the company of white folks, a forbidden society for Dallas Potter, and had threatened anyone who dared to interfere. Colfax had, in effect, dared Pullman society to do something about it, and one of them had accepted the dare. For the first time in his life, Colfax felt genuine, biting guilt. *I killed him,* he told himself, *as sure as if I had wielded the blade.*

But he had to shake off those kinds of thoughts. He had to concentrate on finding the killer. What did he have to go on? Not much. Sometime after the final curtain, probably after everyone else had left the theater, the killer went into the building and found Potter in his dressing room. He had probably arrived just in the nick of time, for Potter had already changed out of his costume and was dressed again to go out into the street. The killer had taken Potter by surprise and brutally murdered him, maybe with a sharp hunting knife. Then after hacking the body savagely, the killer had dragged it down the hallway and outside the building. Why? Had he intended to carry the body off and dispose of it? If so, perhaps he had heard someone coming. Perhaps he'd been interrupted and forced to abandon his original plan. He apparently had his horse waiting there for a quick escape, so when he was interrupted, he'd dropped the body, jumped on his horse, and made good his escape. He'd ridden off to the west, but his horse's tracks had been soon lost in those of the town's traffic.

It could have been anyone. Enough time had passed for someone who had been in the audience to have left with everyone else and returned, but it could as easily have been someone who had not seen the play. And what about motive? No one in Pullman knew Dallas Potter. Colfax had only the one suggestion—race—and already he knew that on that basis he had perhaps eighty percent of the population of the valley as suspects. The only real clue so far was the bloody right boot print with the slashed sole, and how in the hell was he going to find the boot that had left it? Well, he decided, he couldn't just wander around the countryside looking at bootprints, and he was being paid by Tiff Lanagan to do a job. He would have to concentrate on Lanagan's problem and content himself with keeping himself open and alert to anything that might appear to him along the way that might help in the other case. It would not be easy, but that was the way he would have to play.

It was late evening before Rondo Hughes returned to Pullman and found Colfax in his room at the Railhead. Colfax gestured toward the chair as he sat on the edge of the bed.

"Sit down, Mr. Hughes," he said. "What did you find?"

"Well," said Hughes, "it took me awhile, going around the long way like I done, but I did sure enough find a kind of a dry wash up there a ways beyond Youngblood's camp. There's been some cattle in there recent like, but there ain't none in there now."

"Many?"

"Naw. Just a few. It looks to me like Youngblood and them probably herded what strays they could round up into that little wash to hold them until they could take them off and sell them."

Colfax stood up and paced the floor. He took out his makings and rolled a cigarette, then offered them to Hughes. While Hughes was rolling his own, Colfax lit his and took a deep draw. Something was wrong. His instinct told him that if there had been stolen cattle from the valley, they had been taken up beyond that cow camp. His trail sense told him that more than a few cows had been driven up the trail that he had ridden with Hughes. If they had not been held in that wash, then where had they been taken?

"Mr. Hughes," he said finally, "I want you to hang around town tomorrow on your own. Spend some time in the saloons. Wherever you can insinuate yourself into local conversation. Don't ask any questions that would make anyone suspicious of your motives. Just talk casually with folks and listen."

"All right, boss," said Hughes, expelling smoke from his lungs, "but just ezackly what is it I'm listening for?"

"Attitudes concerning the murder of Mr. Potter. I want to know how people feel about it. I want to know what people think about."

"Tiff Lanagan paying you to investigate that nigger's killing?" asked Hughes.

"Tiff Lanagan is paying me," said Colfax, "but I'm paying you, and that's what I want you to do."

Then under the pretext that he was ready to turn in for the night, Colfax sent Hughes on his way. He listened at the door to the cowboy's footsteps as they faded down the hallway; then he strapped on his Colt. He picked up his big coat, for he knew that up in the mountains at night the cold could be bitter, even this time of year. He grabbed his Winchester carbine, put on his hat, and moved to the door. Opening the door only slightly, he peered out into the hallway. He saw no one. He stepped out, shut and locked the door behind himself, and walked down the hallway—not toward the stairway which led down into the hotel lobby, but in the opposite direction. The hallway led to a window which Colfax opened. Below the window was a small landing with a narrow stairway leading down into the alley—a fire escape. Unseen, he made his way down the stairs, down the alley, and around to the stable. Soon he was riding toward the mountains.

Woodward Granger and Tyndall Tabor not only played the parts of the inseparable and amoral brothers in *Titus Andronicus,* they had become in real life practically inseparable. Like all the cast members, they were suffering from frayed nerves as a result of the murder. They were also suffering from intense boredom waiting to find out what Adrian Channing was going to do about the remainder of their western tour. Between them, they had a few dollars, so they decided to check out some of the local saloons. Soon they found themselves at a small bar called Hiram's, at the far eastern end of the main street of Pullman. They bought a bottle of Cyrus Noble whiskey, and took it with two glasses to a table nearby. Granger looked around the small barroom a bit nervously as Tabor poured two drinks.

"Cheers," said Tabor.

They clinked their glasses together, then tossed down the contents. Tabor poured again.

"Filthy business about Potter," he said.

"Talk about something else," said Granger. "Just thinking about that makes my skin crawl."

Granger tossed down his second drink and pushed his glass toward Tabor, who refilled it.

"Go a bit slow, Woody," he said. "The night is yet young."

"Yeah," said Granger, taking a sip from his own drink. "What's the old man going to do?"

"Your guess is as good as mine," said Tabor. "We're already as doubled in the cast as we can get, and we're not likely to find another Aaron the Moor out here in the wild West. He'll have to cancel. That's what I think."

"We could do another play. With a few rehearsals we could do *Macbeth*. We all know those parts. Just a little brushup would be all we need."

"I don't know. We'll find out what he's going to do when he decides, I imagine. Maybe we can suggest it to him if he doesn't come up with it on his own. He looks awfully worn and tired, you know."

"Yes."

Tabor poured two more drinks from the bottle of Cyrus Noble. Back in a corner of the room, Rondo Hughes stood up from a table with a group of cowboys and excused himself. He made his way over to the table where Granger and Tabor sat drinking. Stopping, he touched the brim of his hat.

"Howdy, gents," he said.

"Oh," said Granger, "how do you do? I'm afraid I've forgotten your name."

"It's Hughes. Rondo Hughes. Y'all can just call me Rondo."

"Would you join us, Mr.—uh, Rondo?" said Tabor.

Hughes pulled out a chair and sat down.

"Thank you," he said. He placed the empty glass he had carried with him from the other table down suggestively in front of himself. Tabor pushed the bottle toward Hughes.

"Please help yourself," he said.

Hughes poured himself a drink, then refilled the glasses of the two actors.

"You know," he said, "I never seen a play before. Not until yours. It was pretty damned exciting. Bloody as hell. And it looked real too."

"It turned out to be all too real," said Tabor.

"Tyndall," said Granger. "Please." He tossed his drink down in one gulp and reached for the bottle.

"Sorry," said Tabor with a long sigh.

"Oh, yeah," said Hughes. "That's too bad what happened to your nigger. What y'all going to do now?"

"We don't know," said Granger, "and we, uh, we never really thought of Dallas—that way."

"He was a fine actor," said Tabor, "and a good friend. It's a terrible loss to all of us."

Granger emptied his glass again, then leaned back in his chair and put a hand to his forehead.

"Oh," he said, "I'm afraid that I've passed my limit."

"You okay, buddy?" said Hughes.

"No. Not really. I'd better get myself back to the hotel and go to bed. I'm afraid I may be ill."

Tabor stood up.

"I'll take you back," he said.

"No, no," said Granger. "I can make it all right. There's no need for you to cut short your evening just because I'm drunk. I'll make it."

"You're sure?" said Tabor.

"Of course," said Granger, drawing himself up straight and assuming as much dignity as he could manage. "Besides you still have whiskey in the bottle, and it mustn't go to waste. You two enjoy it. Good night."

As Granger staggered out the door, Hughes twisted in his chair to watch the man's progress.

"He'll be all right," said Tabor. "He doesn't drink very well, I'm afraid. A fine fellow otherwise."

"He seems a mite nervous to me," said Hughes.

"We all are. After all, one of our company has just been murdered in this town."

"Oh, I wouldn't let that bother me if I was you," said Hughes. He tossed down his drink and reached for the bottle. "Y'all are white."

It was late when Tyndall Tabor said good night to Rondo Hughes and left Hiram's to return to the hotel. He was a bit unsteady on his feet, but he didn't stagger the way Granger had. Tabor took pride in his ability to handle the booze. On the stairway in the hotel he slowed down some and had to hang on to the banister and even pull himself up the stairs. He stopped on the landing to catch his breath, then reeled down the hallway to the room he shared with Woodward Granger. He fumbled with the key and dropped it on the floor. Bending to retrieve it, he noticed a faint light coming out under the door. The drunken fool, he said to himself. He's gone to sleep and left the lamp burning. He stood up and started to unlock the door but found that it was already unlocked.

"Damn," he mumbled, as he opened the door. He stepped inside the room and looked up, then stopped. There before him in the faint light from the lamp on the table was Granger. He was lying in bed under the sheet. His eyes were wide open, his lower jaw hanging, and a horrible gash across his throat had let a vast amount of blood run down and soak into the sheets.

"God," said Tabor. "Oh, God." He stepped closer to the bed in horrid fascination. He reached a hand out toward the bloody body but withdrew it with a twitch before it had touched anything. "Oh, my God. Woody."

Tabor took two faltering steps backward, then turned to rush from the room, but as he turned he saw a figure step out from behind the open door and step toward him. He started to scream, but the impact of the man's fist in his stomach stopped the noise.

It knocked the wind out of him, and then he felt the deeper pain. It had been more than a fist. He looked down and just before his world started reeling and turning black, he saw the knife which was buried in his flesh.

Chapter Nine

It had been a long and cold ride, but Colfax had managed to find his way around both the home of the Wheelers and the camp of Youngblood, and though he had never been there before and it was dark, he believed that he had found the dry wash that Rondo Hughes had told him about. He had used most of the night in getting there, and he couldn't tell anything in the dark, so he settled down to wait for the light. He wanted to find out if Youngblood had any cattle up there. If so, he wanted to look at their brands. If not, he wanted to know if there had been any held there recently. He wasn't at all sure what his next move would be if he failed to find any real evidence up here in the draw.

As the sun began to cast light over the rocks, Colfax, leaving his black mare, walked down into the wash. There were no cattle there. He hadn't expected any, for even in the dark had there been cattle in any significant numbers, he would surely have heard them or smelled them. No cattle. There was, however, plenty of evidence that a fairly good sized herd had been there recently. Probably, Colfax figured on the basis of the tracks and the droppings, they had been moved out only in the last day or so. He wondered what would have made Youngblood and his bunch move their cows out at just this time. Maybe his presence in the area had made them panic. Maybe he shouldn't have been so open about his mission. Perhaps if he had been secretive about his reason for being in the valley, he might have been able to catch them off guard. But no, he decided. His reputation would have precluded that. His presence alone would have alerted them.

Colfax did not think that anyone was around, but he felt vulnerable there in the open. Besides, there was nothing to be seen in the wash. Cattle had been there and had been moved recently. He made his way back to the black mare and mounted her, then began to backtrack his own trail. The going was much easier in the daylight, and it wasn't long before Colfax had ridden as far as he wanted to go. He dismounted and tied the black to some brush. If he had calculated right, he should be just due north of the Youngblood camp. He could cut through the brushy foothills and come up on the blind side of the encampment. He would have to go slow and easy. It was noisy traveling through the brush and on the rocks, and he wasn't exactly sure about the route. He had only guessed that he had started more or less due north of the camp. And he wasn't sure how far from the camp he would be, even if he did make a straight shot at it. He had ridden at least a mile north of the trail that led to Youngblood's before heading up into the hills the night before, but the chances were slim that the two trails ran anything like parallel to each other. He could have a mile to walk, or a quarter of a mile. Colfax was a skilled outdoorsman, but he knew that, at best, outdoorsmanship was an inexact science.

The sun climbed higher into the sky, and soon Colfax was glad that he had left the big coat back on his saddle. He had also left the Winchester. It would be of little use to him in the thick brush and on the rugged terrain through which he was painstakingly making his way, and it would be cumbersome. He moved slowly, stopping and listening frequently. He was on ground totally unfamiliar to him. When the ground suddenly began to slope downward in front of him, he knew that he was either getting close to the river or he had inadvertently changed direction and was moving east, down the mountain. He squinted up into the sky to check the position of the sun. He believed that he was moving in the right direction. Then he saw the smoke.

He looked around for a better vantage point, spied a large rock just to his right, and scampered up on top of it. It was the cow camp, all right. The smoke was coming from a small fire out in front of the tent on the north side of the river. Colfax could see only one cowboy moving around the camp. From where he perched, he could see no horses. He eased himself back down off the rock and began picking his way toward the camp. Working harder to stay as quiet as possible the nearer he got to the camp, Colfax soon felt the strain. He was sweating freely, and his muscles began to grow weary. He knew that they would ache later. It crossed his mind that he was getting too old for this. Once again he told himself that after this round, it would be quitting time.

He moved in as close as he dared to the camp. The cowboy was absentmindedly tossing a penknife at a piece of cordwood which lay on the ground. He was standing so that his back was toward Colfax. He tossed the knife, which failed to stick in the wood and fell to the ground. The cowboy bent to pick up his knife from the dirt, and Colfax got a glimpse of his face. It was Denny Doyle. Doyle wiped the blade of his knife on his trouser leg, then faced the tent.

"J.C.," he yelled.

So there was at least one other in the camp. There was no answer, though, and Doyle hollered again.

"J.C., what the hell are you doing in there?"

J. C. Butler emerged from the tent.

"None of your damn business," he said.

"I'm getting bored," said Doyle. "I don't know why we had to stay here anyhow."

"'Cause Youngblood said we ought," said Butler. "That's why."

Doyle flipped his knife at the stick of wood and missed.

"But them cows had to be moved fast. They had to be moved fast. That's what Rondo said. And if the two of us had went along, we could've helped them all along faster. Ain't that right?"

Rondo Hughes, thought Colfax. So he's in with them for sure. Colfax had hired Hughes because of his claim to have been formerly associated with the Youngblood bunch. He had not believed the man's claim that he had left the group, and he had not disbelieved him. He had just decided that it might be handy to have him around, and he had always kept him in sight. The act Hughes had put on for him with Youngblood and the rest the day of the pretended ambush had been a good one, and Colfax had about made up his mind that Hughes was straight, but then Hughes had gotten careless. Colfax had sent him up the mountain alone to follow the cow tracks, and Hughes had said that only a few head had been driven up into the wash. Colfax knew then that something was wrong with Hughes. He had seen the tracks on the trail himself. Now he knew. There was no more question. Rondo Hughes was still working with Youngblood, and they were the rustlers.

"Denny," said Butler, "you got a fuss with Youngblood, you tell him about it, all right? I don't give a shit one way or the other, long as I get my cut."

They were guilty, thought Colfax. There was no doubt about it now. Maybe he didn't have the kind of evidence that would hold up in a court of law, but then, he didn't give a damn about that. He had enough to convince himself, and that was what mattered to Colfax. He might as well go ahead and take these two, and he'd best do it now, while they were both standing there close together. He eased the Colt out of its holster. He'd have to take about ten steps, he figured, to get into a position where he could adequately cover both men, and they would have to be quiet steps.

"Well, what the hell are we supposed to do out here while we wait for them to get back? Huh?" said Doyle.

Butler started walking back toward the tent.

"Where the hell are you going now?" said Doyle.

"I don't want to listen to your bellyaching."

Colfax moved fast. He no longer had a choice, but his crashing through the brush alerted the two cowboys. Butler made a dive for a rifle which leaned against the tent, and Colfax made a split-second decision. He stopped, pointed the Colt at Butler, and squeezed the trigger. Butler had just grabbed the rifle and rolled. He was on his back trying to level the rifle. Both his feet were in the air. The .45 slug caught him in the midsection, and his hands went limp. The rifle fell across his thighs, and he made a vain attempt to sit up. He sat for a ludicrous moment on his butt, his head off the ground, his feet still in the air. Then he fell back and lay still.

But Colfax had turned away from Doyle in order to fire at Butler, and that provided Doyle with all the time he needed to pull his own pistol from his belt and fire a quick shot at Colfax. The bullet burned through Colfax's flesh on the left side just above his belt. He spun toward the pain, and a second bullet whizzed past his head. He dropped to his left knee, pointed the Colt, and fired. Doyle made a sound as if all his breath had been knocked out of him as the heavy .45 slug smashed through his sternum. He looked down at the wound, surprised; then he sank slowly to his knees. His right hand was still out in front of him, but the fingers slowly relaxed, and the six-gun fell to the ground. Doyle sat down on his feet, swayed a moment, then fell over on his right side.

Colfax waited a moment, watching the camp and listening. He saw no movement, heard nothing. The gash along his side was burning. It felt like a red-hot iron had been jabbed through his flesh. He reached down and gripped the wound with his left hand and felt the blood running through his fingers. He walked into the camp and looked at the two bodies. Then he looked around. Two horses were in a makeshift corral downhill from the tent. He decided to take a quick look inside the tent. There he found fresh beef, and over in a corner, a cowhide. They had apparently slaughtered one for food before driving off the others. He moved to the hide and gave it a quick inspection. There, with no evidence of even an attempt to alter it, was Tiff Lanagan's brand. He picked up the cowhide and got out of the tent. He stood there for a moment, trying to decide his next move.

His horse was too far away and too hard to get to. He was already feeling weak and light-headed. The burning sensation in his left side had begun to give way to a heavy throbbing, each throb accompanied by a dull, sickening pain. He felt like he was going to puke. The Wheelers. He could get to the Wheelers more quickly and easily than he could to the black mare. He started to walk down the trail. What was he thinking? There were two horses in the corral. The horses of the two men he had just killed. He could take one of them. There was a gray and a dun in the corral, both mares. The dun was a little larger but showed signs of ill use. Colfax chose the smaller gray. Two saddles were hung across the top rail of the corral. He dragged one off the rail and pain shot through his side. Somehow he managed to get the saddle onto the gray and himself up into the saddle without passing out. He took a few deep breaths, then headed the gray down the trail.

He knew that the trail was steep, but he hadn't realized before just how steep it really was. He had to lean back in the saddle to keep from losing his balance, and when he did that, it felt as if he were being ripped apart there at his left side just above the belt. The throbbing continued, and the dull, sick feeling at the pit of his stomach grew more intense. As he estimated that he had made it about halfway down to the Wheeler place, he began to feel drowsy. He was afraid that he would go to sleep or pass out before he reached his destination. He vaguely wondered how much blood he had lost. He wondered if the bleeding had stopped or if his body was continuing to be drained. He had no sense of what was happening with the wound other than his too-acute sense of the incessant throbbing.

He wondered with what little consciousness he had remaining just how he would be received by the Wheelers. His instinct told him that they were not involved with the Hughes-Youngblood gang, but Tiff Lanagan was convinced that they were. Neither

Colfax nor Lanagan had any real way of knowing, but then, he didn't really see that he had much choice at this point. He might make it to the Wheelers. He knew that he could not make it to Lanagan's, or to Pullman, or to Dierks's. He certainly could not have made it back to his black mare.

He was nearly unconscious when the mare walked up to the Wheeler house, and he would have let her walk right on by had it not been for Tommy Wheeler. Tommy was out in front of the house splitting wood, and he looked up as Colfax approached. He smiled a big, friendly smile.

"Hi," he said. "Hey. You all right?"

When Colfax didn't answer, Tommy ran to grab the reins of the gray mare and stop her. Colfax reeled in the saddle.

"You're hurt," said Tommy.

He reached up to try to pull Colfax down from the saddle, just as the door to the cabin opened and Mrs. Wheeler stepped out.

"Tommy," she said, "who is it?"

"It's that man that came to see us," said Tommy. "He's hurt."

Tommy's sister-in-law ran out to help, and soon the two of them had Colfax out of the saddle and into the house. The other two Wheelers were not around. As Colfax felt himself being lowered onto a bed, he struggled to bring himself more fully to consciousness.

"My horse," he said.

"Don't you worry about your horse, mister," said Tommy. "I'll take care of it for you."

"No," said Colfax. "Listen. That's not my horse. Get rid of it. I got it—up the mountain."

"Youngblood and them," said Mrs. Wheeler. "Is that where you got hurt?"

"Two of them," said Colfax. "One shot me. I got them both."

"When they come back by here, they'll see that horse," said Mrs. Wheeler.

"There's another trail," said Colfax. "North."

"I know it," said Tommy.

"Take that gray over there. My horse is there. A black. Take the black to Lanagan's. Tell him—"

Colfax's world suddenly vanished into a swirling blackness, and he knew no more.

"What's he mean?" asked Tommy.

"He left a black horse on the other trail. He must have walked over to Youngblood's. He killed two of them up there and got shot. He wants you to take this gray horse over to get his horse. Then ride his horse down to Tiff Lanagan's ranch and tell Mr. Lanagan where he's at. I think that's what he wants. Do you understand all that, Tommy?"

Tommy looked puzzled and scratched his head. Then a smile broke out over his young face.

"Yeah," he said. "I can do that. That horse out there ain't really his. His horse is over there on the north trail."

"That's right."

"I ride this horse over to get his horse."

"Yes."

Tommy looked puzzled again.

"What do I do with this horse?" he said.

"Oh, I don't know, Tommy. Turn it loose over there. Okay?"

"Okay. Then I ride down to Lanagan's and tell Mr. Lanagan that this man is here. Right?"

"That's right. Now go. We don't want none of that Youngblood bunch to come riding by here and see that horse."

"Dora?"

Dora Wheeler was putting some water on the stove to heat. Her patience was wearing thin.

"What?" she said.

"What do I do next? After that?"

"After that just come on back home. Now go."

Tommy ran to the door and opened it. Then he turned back to face Dora.

"I'll do it," he said, and he ran out, leaving the door open behind him. Dora Wheeler rushed to the door to shut it, then rushed back to her other business.

"God," she said. "I hope he don't die here."

The blackness that had engulfed the world of Oliver Colfax soon turned to red, a deep, blood red, and Colfax was swimming in it. He wasn't swimming, really, not the way a man swims through water, purposefully, deliberately. It was more like he was caught in an eddy and was being whirled through the thick red, and as the pool spun him round and dragged him ever deeper, he began to catch fleeting glimpses of others—other people caught in the same swirl. There was Adrian Channing. No. It wasn't Channing at all. It was Titus Andronicus himself, his mouth wide open in a hideous scream, but no noise came forth. Then Titus was gone, as quickly as he had appeared, and there was Aaron, his mouth, too, gaping wide, but Aaron wasn't screaming. He was laughing. He was laughing at first, but then he changed, and he was no longer Aaron. He was Dallas Potter, the black actor, and his laughter turned to a cry, but still there was no sound, and still Colfax turned, or the world, the red world, turned round him.

He saw the bloody and pitiful Lavinia, and he saw again the blood splatter as he shot first J. C. Butler, then Denny Doyle, and throughout all this, there was the constant, painful, rhythmic throbbing, which came from his left side but which resounded in his head and pounded, too, deep in his groin. And then the faces vanished, the red deepened and turned again to black, the swirling slowed and finally stopped, and Colfax slipped slowly and mercifully into an all-encompassing oblivion.

Chapter Ten

Tommy Wheeler rode hard. He felt a sense of urgency, first because the man for whom he was riding had been shot, second because Dora's voice had been urgent, and finally because he felt somehow that his brothers would disapprove of what he was doing. They had often told him to stay away from the Lanagan spread. This time Dora had told him to go, so it should be all right. Still, he wanted to get it over with. He had ridden cross-country from the trail which passed by his house to the other one farther north, and he had found the black mare without any trouble at all. He was proud of himself. And he had turned loose the gray that belonged, he guessed, to someone up at Youngblood's place. He was glad to be rid of that horse. His brothers had also told him to stay away from Youngblood and his friends. Tommy didn't quite know why he was to stay clear of all those people. He just had a sense that the Youngblood bunch were bad men and that Lanagan for some reason or other didn't like the Wheelers.

He had turned loose the gray and mounted the big, black horse. It was just waiting there, saddled and ready to go, and it had a rifle on its side. Tommy had whipped up the big mare and started it going as fast as he dared down the trail. It was a powerful horse, fast. It scared him at first, but then he got control of it, got used to its gait. Tommy was good with horses, so his initial fright hadn't lasted long. It had, in fact, turned quickly to a kind of exhilaration. At the bottom of the grade, where the foothills abruptly turned to flat prairie, Tommy pulled back on the reins to slow the mare so she wouldn't stumble. She moved out onto the flat, and he spurred her again to pick up her stride. There was nothing now between him and Lanagan. He had to hurry up and get there and get this over with.

"Come on, you old horse," he shouted. "Come on."

He was amazed at the speed and power of the black mare and at the quickness with which he found himself on Lanagan range. Then up ahead he saw two cowboys. They were riding along at a leisurely pace, coming toward him. Then they appeared to notice him. They moved aside, for he was headed right toward them. He felt a sudden sense of panic. They must be Lanagan cowboys. They shouted something at him, but he couldn't understand the words for the wind in his ears. He was getting close to them. One of the cowboys snaked out a loop. They moved as if they were coming to get him.

"Come on, horse," he shouted, and he spurred the mare's flanks and lashed at her sides with the long, loose ends of the reins. Just as he passed the cowboys by, he saw out of the corner of his eye the one with the loop swing his arm. He saw the flash of the loop. He passed the cowboys, and then he felt the coarse loop fall over his shoulders, felt it tighten and cut into him an instant before it jerked him backward out of the saddle. He flew through the air, and an involuntary scream escaped his lungs. Then he landed with a powerful thud, and he bounced once, high, it seemed, into the air. He landed again and lay still, gasping and choking for air, for everything in his lungs had been knocked out by the impact.

"Go get that black," said the cowboy with the rope.

The other puncher took off after the mare, who, when she realized that something had happened to her load, had begun to slow down in confusion. Tommy tried to get up, but he still hadn't caught his breath, and besides, the cowboy kept the rope taut by backing up his cow pony. When Tommy finally managed to struggle to his feet, still gasping, the drover gave a jerk and pulled him over again. This time he landed hard on his face. The other cowboy rode back leading the black mare.

"It's Mr. Lanagan's horse, all right," he said.

"Yeah," said the roper, "and this here's one of them damn rustlers."

He suddenly let his rope go slack, but he rode up close to Tommy until his horse's hooves were nearly trampling him. The other cowboy took that as his cue and rode up close on Tommy's other side.

"What's your name, boy?" said the roper.

Tommy had just begun to get his breath, and when he answered, he hollered out much more loudly than he had meant to.

"I'm Tommy," he said.

The second drover nudged his mount nearer, and Tommy tried to roll away from the hooves, but the other horse was stamping on the other side. He tried to pull in his shoulders to make himself smaller.

"Tommy what?" said the roper.

"It's Wheeler, ain't it?" said the second drover. "You're one of them Wheelers lives up on the mountain, ain't you?"

"I'm Tommy Wheeler. Yes. Let me go."

The roper backed his horse away a few feet and dismounted, then moved in on Tommy quickly, pulling him roughly to his feet. He held him by the shirtfront.

"What the hell are you doing down here, Tommy Wheeler?" he said.

"I came to see Mr. Lanagan," said Tommy.

"I'll just bet you did," said the roper, giving Tommy a shove. Tommy staggered backward, and the other cowboy caught him and spun him around.

"Where'd you get that horse?" he said.

"The man had it."

"He ain't making no sense, Chalk," said the cowboy.

The roper, the one called Chalk, spun Tommy back around and drove a fist into his stomach. Tommy bent over, his so recently regained breath driven out again. Slobber was drooling from his lower lip, and he was fighting again for his breath. Even in his fear and panic and pain, a thought raced through Tommy's mind. *Lark and Spud are going to be mad at me for this.*

"Let's teach this one what happens to rustlers around here," said Chalk.

The rope had finally come loose and dropped down around Tommy's waist, and about that same instant, Tommy's confusion and fear gave way to anger. His hands were free, and he swung a right from way down low as he straightened himself up. His fist caught Chalk underneath the chin, causing him to stagger back a few steps, but the other cowboy reacted quickly. He drove his right into Tommy's right side. Tommy yelled out in pain and frustration and anger as he whirled, his left making for the cowboy's head, but the cowboy blocked it with his right and punched Tommy in the chest with his left. It staggered Tommy, but only slightly. Tommy swung a right which missed its mark, but his right arm circled the man's head, and Tommy pulled him down into a wrestler's headlock.

Chalk's head had cleared a bit, and he looked up to see what was happening.

"Get the son of a bitch, Carl," he said.

Carl was flailing his arms, and Tommy suddenly threw his right hip out to the side and executed a flying mare on Carl, sending him through the air to land hard at Chalk's feet. Chalk saw that Tommy was still standing in the loop that had fallen from around him, and he moved quickly to grab up the end of the rope and jerk it, sending Tommy over backward. Then he ran over to kick at Tommy's ribs and head. Tommy covered his head with his arms. Carl scrambled to his feet and joined in the same activity as his partner. The kicks aimed at Tommy's head weren't doing much damage, but the ones to the ribs were having much more effect. Chalk stopped kicking and stepped back.

"That's enough," he said.

Carl gave one more swift kick to Tommy's ribs before he stopped.

"Tie his hands behind him," said Chalk, "and let's take him down to the boss. Likely we'll have us a hanging."

They pulled Tommy's hands behind him and tied them with the same rope that Chalk had used to rope him out of the saddle. Then they pulled him to his feet and shoved him up onto the black mare.

Boyd Gruver was just coming out of Lanagan's house when Chalk and Carl came riding up, Tommy on the black mare between them.

"Hey, Boyd," said Chalk, "look what we got here."

Gruver walked up closer to the riders to get a better look. Tommy was sagging in the saddle. Caked blood and dirt covered his head and his clothes were bloodstained.

"That's Tommy Wheeler, ain't it?" said Gruver.

"Yeah," said Carl. "Look what he's riding. We caught him going across our range lickety-split."

"What'd you do to him?" said Gruver.

"Aw, hell," said Chalk, "we just kicked him around a little. He wouldn't tell us where he got the horse."

"But we knowed that he'd stole it," said Carl.

"I told them," said Tommy, but his voice was weak and Gruver heard only a whine.

"What? What did you say?"

"I told them," said Tommy, his voice a little stronger than before. "I come to see Mr. Lanagan."

Gruver looked at Carl, then at Chalk.

"Did he tell you that?"

"Yeah," said Chalk, "I think he did say something about wanting to see the boss."

"Then why the hell didn't you bring him on down here?"

Chalk was holding the end of the rope which bound Tommy's hands behind his back. He looked at Tommy, then back at Gruver, and he tossed the rope down toward Gruver's feet.

"Well, shit," he said. "Here he is."

Carl laughed out loud. Then Chalk pulled his mount around and started off, and Carl followed. Gruver called out to their backs.

"Hey," he said. "Go on back to the bunkhouse and pack your gear. Then you can ride back over here and draw your wages. You're both through."

Chalk stopped his horse and turned back to face Gruver, his face registering genuine amazement.

"For pounding a little on a goddamned rustler?" he said.

"You heard me," said Gruver. He was helping Tommy down out of the saddle, and he could see that Tommy was crying. "Come on, boy," he said. "It'll be all right. We'll get you cleaned up here in a minute."

"I have to see Mr. Lanagan," said Tommy.

"Okay. First let me get these damn ropes off of you. Okay? Then we'll go in the house. Mr. Lanagan's in the house."

Tiff Lanagan sprang to his feet as he saw Gruver come into the house propping up the battered Tommy Wheeler.

"Good God," he said. "What's happened?"

"It's Tommy Wheeler," said Gruver. "Chalk and Carl caught him on our range riding your black mare."

"He told me to ride it," said Tommy. "I didn't steal it. He told me to."

"Who told you, Tommy?" said Gruver.

"That man. The one who came to see us. He ate dinner with us. I don't know his name. I can't remember. He's hurt."

Lanagan caught Tommy by an arm and led him to a chair.

"So are you," he said. "Just sit down here." He turned and called out over his shoulder, "Agnes. Agnes, come in here."

"I didn't do nothing wrong," said Tommy.

"All right," said Lanagan. "All right. Just take it easy."

Agnes Lanagan stepped into the room.

"Agnes," said Lanagan, "we need to clean this boy up and see how bad he might be hurt."

"I'll be right back," she said.

"Mr. Lanagan, I came to see you," said Tommy. "They told me to."

"Who told you to, son?"

"Dora and the man."

"What man are you talking about? The man who rode the black horse?"

"Yeah. Him. He got shot, and he came to my house. Dora's helping him."

"Colfax?" said Boyd Gruver. "Are you talking about Colfax?"

"Yeah," said Tommy. "Colfax. That's his name. I remember now. I think. Colfax."

Agnes Lanagan came back into the room with a basin of warm water and a rag.

"Now get out of my way," she said.

Lanagan and Gruver each stepped to one side of the big chair, and Agnes started to work on the dirty and battered face.

"Oh, you poor boy," she said.

Tommy winced as she wiped at the caked blood on his temple.

"I'm all growed," he said. "Everyone calls me boy anyhow, though."

"You say Colfax is at your house and he's been shot?" said Lanagan.

"Yeah. Got shot. He told me to get his black horse and bring it here and see you."

Tommy had begun to talk, and it seemed nothing would stop him. He babbled on even while Agnes Lanagan continued daubing at his scrapes and bruises.

"He wants you to come out to see him. He told me to bring you. Colfax. Dora told me, too. They said to hurry. I think he killed two of them. Yeah. Two."

"Who?" said Lanagan. "Who did he kill?"

"Two of them guys with Youngblood. Two of them. I don't know their names."

"Hush now," said Agnes. "Mr. Lanagan will take care of it. You just rest easy and let me finish here."

"Lark will be mad at me. So will Spud."

"Your brothers?" said Agnes. "Why will they be mad at you?"

"They told me to stay away from here. They said—"

"What, Tommy?" said Agnes. "What did they say? It's all right. You can tell me."

Tommy looked at Agnes, then at Lanagan and Gruver. Agnes wiped at his face some more.

"They said that he don't like us," said Tommy, and his eyes were on Tiff Lanagan.

"That's not true, Tommy," said Agnes. "We like you just fine. You seem like a very nice young man to me."

"Well, they beat me up. They roped me and beat me up. They work for him, don't they?"

Agnes looked at Lanagan, her eyes pleading with him to say something that might make a difference to Tommy Wheeler. Boyd Gruver saved the situation.

"I fired them two, Tommy," he said. "Mr. Lanagan didn't know they was going to do that, and they shouldn't have done it. I fired them."

Lanagan looked at Gruver, surprised.

"Good," he said. "You saved me the trouble."

"Yeah," said Tommy, his face wrinkled in deep thought. "Yeah. That's right. I remember now. I heard you. He fired them two guys. They shouldn't do that. They shouldn't hurt people. It ain't right."

"No, Tommy, it's not right," said Agnes. "Well, I think that's about all I can do for you now. I don't think anything's broken. You're just cut and bruised is all. You're going to be just fine."

"Can you ride now?" said Lanagan.

"Sure," said Tommy. "I'm going to be just fine." He looked at Agnes and smiled.

"Good," said Lanagan. "We're going with you. Me and Boyd here, and a couple of cowboys who work for me. We'll get the horses ready. You just wait here, and we'll be ready in a minute."

Lanagan and Gruver walked out onto the porch in time to see Chalk and Carl coming back to the house. They had their blanket rolls tied on behind their saddles. Lanagan gave Gruver a questioning look.

"I told them to pack up and come back over here for their wages," said Gruver.

Lanagan pulled a wallet out of his coat pocket, thumbed through a few bills, and handed some to Gruver.

"That cover it?" he asked.

"It's more than they got coming to them."

"Well, give it to them, and good riddance."

Gruver walked off the porch to meet the two cowboys. Lanagan stood aloof from the proceedings and watched as Gruver handed each cowboy some bills. Chalk snatched his from Gruver's hand, then looked at Lanagan.

"You going along with this, Mr. Lanagan?" he asked.

"Boyd's foreman," said Lanagan.

"We caught that kid red-handed. He was on one of your horses."

"Did you bother to ask him how he come by it?" snapped Lanagan. "That poor boy's a half-wit, Chalk. Even if his brothers are rustlers, there's no excuse for two men beating up on a half-wit kid like that. Now get off my range before I decide to have you both horsewhipped. If you know what's good for you, you'll get plumb out of the valley."

Lanagan walked to where the black mare stood, still saddled and panting. He put a hand on its side.

"Boyd, get someone to take care of this horse, and get two good men to ride with us. Saddle five horses."

"Yes, sir," said Gruver, and he headed off at a trot. Lanagan watched him from the porch. He stroked his chin and found it rough. He had forgotten to shave that morning.

"Damn," he said out loud. He turned and walked back into the house.

Chapter Eleven

Tiff Lanagan called a halt to his men in front of the Wheeler house. With him were Boyd Gruver, Tommy Wheeler, and two cowboys called Link and Billy O. There at the front door of the cabin stood Lark and Spud. Lark held an old seven-shot Spencer carbine, Spud, a sawed-off American Arms 12-gauge shotgun.

"Just take it easy, boys," said Lanagan.

Spud raised the shotgun. He was looking at Tommy. Then his eyes shifted to stare hard at Lanagan.

"What happened to my brother?" he said.

"A couple of my cowboys caught him on my range and beat him up," said Lanagan. "They've been fired."

"I'm sorry, Lark," said Tommy. "I know you told me not to go there."

"It's okay, Tommy. Dora told you to go. I know," said Lark. "You had a reason. Now come on down off or your horse and come over here."

"You ain't mad at me?"

"No, I ain't mad. Come on over here."

Tommy dismounted slowly and walked hesitantly over to stand by Lark's side. He turned and looked back at the four mounted men.

"I ought to kill you, Lanagan, while you're sitting here," said Spud.

"Shut up, Spud," Lark snapped. "What happened, Tommy?"

"They roped me and beat me up," said Tommy, "just like he said. Then they got fired, and she washed my face and fixed me up."

"Who?"

"The lady. She was nice."

"He's referring to my wife," said Lanagan.

"What did you come up here for?" said Lark.

"Your brother said I was asked to come up here. He said that Colfax is inside—shot."

"The son of a bitch is in there, all right," said Spud.

"You need three men with you?" asked Lark.

"You never know."

Lark lowered the carbine. He looked at Tommy and put a hand on the back of the young man's head.

"You okay?" he asked.

"Yeah. Hell, Lark, I'm okay."

"Put the shotgun away, Spud," said Lark. He handed the carbine to Tommy. "Put this away for me, will you? Lanagan, you all climb on down. You can put your horses in there."

Lanagan and the three cowboys led their horses to the small corral toward which Lark Wheeler had gestured. Then, while Billy O. and Link lounged nervously around the corral, Lanagan, followed closely by Gruver, walked over to Lark Wheeler.

"Your man's in there asleep," said Lark. "He ain't hurt bad, I don't think, but he's bled a lot. He'll take some rest to get back in shape."

"What happened?" asked Lanagan.

"I wasn't here. Dora—that's my wife—she said that he come down here shot up. Told her he'd killed two men up the hill. The shot raked him along the side. Dora, she put a poultice on it. That's all I know."

"If Colfax went gunning for those men up there," said Lanagan, "then he must be satisfied they're rustlers. And if you helped him and sent your brother down to my place for help, then I'm satisfied that you're not. I owe you an apology, Wheeler. Not many men have ever got one of them out of me."

The front door opened and Dora stepped out. She was wiping her hands on a thin, faded towel.

"You Mr. Lanagan?" she said.

"I am."

"He's awake, your Mr. Colfax."

Wheeler turned to hold the door open.

"Come on in, Lanagan," he said.

Lanagan followed Dora Wheeler into the cabin. Spud was sitting at the table, scowling. Tommy was at a chair against the far wall with a rag, dusting off his boots. Colfax was in the bed against the wall to Lanagan's right as he came into the room. Lanagan looked around, then walked to the bed.

"How are you?" he said.

"I'll be all right," said Colfax, "thanks to these people."

"What happened?"

"That bunch up the hill are your rustlers, all right. No question about it. I had a cowhide that I found up there."

"It's outside," said Tommy. "You want me to get it?"

"Thanks, Tommy," said Colfax. "Give it to Mr. Gruver. Anyhow, they've moved a bunch of cows out of there just lately. They're the ones. These folks here, the Wheelers, they're clean."

"I figured that," said Lanagan. "So you're satisfied that we got the goods on Youngblood and his bunch?"

"I'm satisfied."

"All right, Colfax," said Lanagan. "Then that's good enough for me. You want us to take you down to the ranch?"

"He'd better not go yet," said Dora. "He ought to rest up a bit more. Maybe in the morning."

Colfax looked at his nurse and smiled. He did feel weak yet, and the pain still burned in his side.

"She's probably right," he said. "I'll get up and head down there in the morning. If I make it all right, I'll get back to work tomorrow afternoon."

"Well," said Lanagan, "there's no hurry on that. Don't rush it. I want to leave a couple of men here until you come down. Is that all right with you, Wheeler?"

"What the hell for?" said Spud Wheeler before Lark had the chance to answer.

"What if Youngblood and that bunch comes back and finds him here?" said Lanagan. "What'll they do to you if they find Colfax here and he's just gunned two of their cronies?"

"He's right, Spud," said Lark. "If it was just me and you, I'd say to hell with them, but I don't want to take no chances with Dora and Tommy here."

"Youngblood and them won't be back for another day or two," said Spud.

Lanagan turned on Spud. Apparently a little suspicion of the Wheelers still lingered in his mind, and Spud's remark triggered it.

"How do you know that?" he said.

"We don't know," said Lark. "But we've seen them head out with cattle before, and each time they've been gone at least four days. Judging from the past, Spud's probably right. But like I said, we can't be sure. I'd appreciate you leaving your men here."

"Hell," said Spud, "there's only four of them left. Colfax killed two of them."

"Five," said Colfax. "I almost forgot to mention something. Rondo Hughes is one of them."

"Goddamn," said Boyd Gruver, who had remained silent up until then, "I knew it. I knew it all along."

"Let's go, Boyd," said Lanagan. "Colfax, we'll look for you tomorrow at the ranch."

Gruver left, and Lanagan had followed him almost out the

door. He stopped and turned back to face Colfax again.

"Oh, yeah," he said. "There's been more killing in town. Two more of them actors. Granger and, uh, Tabor, I think their names was. Just thought you'd want to know."

Granger and Tabor. So Potter wasn't killed because he was black. Someone's killing actors. Potter just happened to be the first one. Colfax struggled to assimilate the new information with what he already had in his mind. He would have to take a new aim. Killing actors. Who would want to kill actors? It didn't make any sense. But Potter, Granger, and Tabor. Three actors murdered. *Damn,* he thought, *I never considered that possibility. I was off on the wrong track right from the start.* Then another thought came to him. If someone was out there murdering actors, there were a number of actors left in Pullman who could become the next victims. He needed to get back to Pullman, had to warn them, to try to protect those who remained. Dort sure wasn't going to be any help, not really. He raised himself up on his right elbow and tried to sit up, but the pain flashed through his body and a sudden burst of red light filled his field of vision.

"Ah," he shouted, as he fell back into the pillow.

"Damn fool," said Lark Wheeler. He was alongside his wife, Dora, within seconds after they heard Colfax shout with pain. "Trying to get up like that."

Dora put a hand on Colfax's forehead. She and Lark stood quietly for a moment, watching and listening.

"He's asleep now," she said.

"Asleep, hell," said Lark. "He's passed out."

Lark walked to the door and opened it.

"Where you going?" asked Dora.

"Just outside, Dora. You need anything, just holler." He went out and pulled the door shut behind himself. Link and Billy O. were leaning against the corral fence looking as if they felt lost. He walked over to join them.

"Billy O.," said Lark. "How you doing?"

"Oh, can't complain none, Lark."

"I ain't never met your pal here."

"Oh. Well, this here's Link Calvin. He's a Texan. Pretty good cowboy, for a Texan."

"Shit," said Link, drawing the word out into three syllables.

Wheeler extended his hand, and the Texan shook it.

"So you boys got left here to wet-nurse Colfax, huh?"

"I reckon," said Billy O.

"Well, just make yourselves at home. We'll have some fresh coffee out here directly. When suppertime comes around, you all will eat with us."

"Thanks, Lark. That's good of you, considering the way the old man has treated you all this time," said Billy O.

Lark Wheeler leaned back against the top rail of the fence, lining up with the two other cowboys.

"That's all behind us now," he said. He reached into a shirt pocket and produced a sack of Bull Durham and a package of papers and offered them to Billy O. Billy O. took them, peeled off a paper, and poured some tobacco into it, then passed them on to Link, who also indulged before returning them to their owner. Soon the three cowboys were smoking.

"Say, Wheeler," said Link. "Do you really think that Youngblood bunch won't make it back before we get Colfax down the hill?"

"I don't think they will. You never know, though."

"That's right," said Billy O., "you never know."

Wheeler took a long drag on his cigarette.

"If they do come back before then," he said, "I don't want anyone here getting killed if we can avoid it. Chances are, if they come riding by here, they'll keep right on going. They don't actually come making social calls very often."

"Maybe you're right," said Billy O. "I'll just be glad when we get him on down the hill."

Lark Wheeler took a last drag off his cigarette and tossed it away.

"You won't be half as glad as I will," he said.

Chapter Twelve

Youngblood and his crew did not return by the next morning, and Colfax felt much stronger after he had had a good, long night's sleep and a meal prepared for him by Dora. Billy O. and Link had taken Colfax back down to the Lanagan ranch, and Agnes Lanagan had a spare bedroom ready for him when they arrived. Colfax was put back to bed in spite of his protests. But the ride down the hill had tired Colfax more than he realized, and he hadn't been back in bed long before he was asleep again. He slept most of that day away, and the following morning he felt like he should be up and back to work. At his request, Agnes Lanagan had a bath prepared for him, and after bathing, he dressed. He was surprised and annoyed that the effort had caused him considerable discomfort and had tired him again. He allowed Agnes to talk him out of leaving the ranch that day.

Just after lunch, which Colfax took at the Lanagan's table, Adrian Channing showed up in the company of his two actresses. They had come to visit Colfax, they said. Agnes saw that they were all seated comfortably and served them coffee. Tiff

Lanagan excused himself. He had work to do, he said, and he left the house.

"We heard that you'd been wounded, Mr. Colfax," said Channing, "and we wanted to see how you are doing. I'm pleased, indeed, to see you doing so well."

"Thank you, Mr. Channing," said Colfax, "but I think that you have more to concern yourself with than my health. From what I've heard, someone in Pullman is murdering actors."

"So they told you," said Channing. "To be honest, I didn't come out here just to inquire about your health. I came to seek your advice. Mr. Colfax, my people are frightened by all this. We don't know what to do. You seem to be a man of—of action. Can you help us?"

Colfax looked at the tired old man, and he felt pity for him. This old Shakespearean actor was faced with real tragic events in his life. He knew tragedy, the old man, but he didn't know how to cope with what was happening to him in Pullman. Colfax couldn't blame him. It was a difficult and puzzling situation.

"Mr. Channing," he said, "I wish I knew what to tell you. When Mr. Potter was murdered, I thought that the killing had been motivated by the color of his skin. I blamed myself, because I had encouraged Mr. Potter to socialize with us in the Railhead, and I figured that some bigot couldn't quite stomach that. But now it seems that someone is just killing actors. That doesn't make sense to me. Why would anyone want to kill actors?"

"Maybe," said Mrs. Dixon Lindsay, "there was a drama critic in the audience."

"Dixon," said Alma Dyer, her voice reproachful.

"A bad joke," said Dixon. "I'm sorry."

"Why don't we just pack up and get out of this place before someone else gets killed?" said Alma.

"That might be a good idea," said Colfax, "except for one thing."

"What's that?" said Channing.

"It doesn't make sense to think that someone out there is just killing actors," said Colfax. "What does make sense is that the killer is someone who knew Potter and Granger and Tabor and had it in for all three for some reason or other."

"Oh," said Channing, "wait a minute, Mr. Colfax. I think I see what you're getting at."

"There's no one in this town who fits that mold except someone in your company," said Colfax.

"One of us?" said Dixon.

"Oh, my God," said Alma.

Channing sagged back in his chair and exhaled a tremendous sigh.

"Of course," he said, "you're right. We have to consider that possibility, as repugnant as it is. It does make a certain amount of sense, and nothing else does. So if we run away, we'd simply be carrying the danger with us on the road. Besides, I really don't want to run away from here and leave this thing unresolved. I'd never feel right about that."

"But who could it be?" said Dixon. "Who among us could—?"

"Has there been any animosity among you?" asked Colfax. "Rivalries? Jealousies? Anything like that you can think of?"

"No, nothing," said Channing. "Well—"

"What, man?" said Colfax. "Nothing is too small to consider."

"Well," said the old man, "Sammy—that is, Samuel Chase, who portrays Saturninus for us—has never quite accepted Dallas Potter. Sammy comes from an old southern family. He used to delight in reminding Dallas that his family had been slave owners."

"That's right," said Dixon. "Remember when he told Dallas, 'Before the war, I could have bought and sold you'?"

"I remember that," said Alma.

"But that wouldn't explain the killings of Granger and Tabor," said Channing.

"Perhaps they saw something or suspected something," said Colfax. "The one real clue we have in this case is a small footprint. I'd say a size seven, eight at the most. It was a boot print, cowboy style, and it had a slash across the sole. The right foot."

"Oh, Lord," said Channing, his face growing visibly whiter.

"Sammy wore boots like that sometimes," said Dixon.

"I don't suppose you'd know his size," said Colfax.

"Of course I do," said Channing. "I have to costume all these people."

The old man sat with a defensive expression on his face. Colfax, Alma Dyer, and Dixon Lindsay all stared at him, waiting. No one had to say anything. He knew what they were waiting for.

"It's seven and a half," he said.

"Oh, God," said Dixon. "It's Sammy."

"Just hold on a minute here," said Colfax. "We don't know that. Not yet. We know that the killer is a man about Sammy's size, and we know that the killer and Sammy both wear cowboy boots."

"And we know that Sammy resented having a black man as his equal," said Dixon.

"We're fairly surrounded here by people who feel that way," said Colfax. "And we're surrounded by men who wear cowboy boots. The size narrows it down a little, but not all that much."

"But you said that it was one of us," said Alma.

"I said that was a possibility. It doesn't look good for Mr. Chase just now, but let's not accuse him just yet. Let's look for more evidence."

Channing stood up and walked to the door. He ran his massive hands through his white hair, then turned and walked back to the chair. He did not sit.

"So," he said, "what do we do?"

"Stay together," said Colfax. "Don't anyone go off alone. And keep your eyes and ears open. Anything you see or hear, anything you think of, let me know about it right away. I'll be doing everything I can to sort this out."

"Thank you, sir," said Channing. "I suppose we had better be getting back to town now. We'll do as you say."

The ladies stood up to leave, and Colfax stood. A pain shot

through his side as he did so. He winced in spite of himself.

"You're still hurting, Mr. Colfax," said Alma Dyer.

"I'm all right, Mrs. Dyer," said Colfax. "Mr. Channing, when I get into town, do you think it would be possible for us, you and me, to get a look at Mr. Chase's belongings without his knowledge? I'd like to see those boots of his."

"Why, yes. I think we could manage that."

As the actors left, Colfax caught himself watching the women. They were lovely creatures, those two. They had beauty, grace, charm, and they were Shakespeareans. What more could any man want? Well, any man like Colfax. Then he chastised himself for his thoughts. He had more urgent things with which to deal. There were the rustlers up on the hill—or wherever they were. They would be back. They had left two of their number behind to guard the camp. Colfax wanted to be ready for them when they returned. His promise to Tiff Lanagan was only half fulfilled. He had found the rustlers. Now he had to stop the rustling. And there was the murderer to seek out.

Even more important was the need to prevent further killings. If Chase had committed the murders, if he had killed Potter because of his prejudice and the other two because they knew, perhaps he would not kill anymore. But if the killer was someone else, someone just killing the actors for some perverse reason, then he could strike again. Colfax felt the need to be out of the house and back on the job. His assistant, Hughes, was one of the rustlers, and the local lawman, Dort, was a joke. There was no one else. Colfax was alone. Lives depended on him. Order depended on him.

He walked out to the corral and found the black Arabian mare. She seemed rested and no worse for wear. The saddle that Colfax had been using was thrown across a fence rail. He considered tossing it on the mare's back, but the pain in his side reminded him that such a move would be a foolish one. He looked around and saw no cowboys. Lanagan had not returned to the ranch house. Oh well, he figured, ranch work keeps men out all day long. Sometimes all night. He was glad it was not his line. He rolled himself a cigarette and lit it. Then he climbed up to sit on the top rail of the corral fence. He had used his right arm to pull himself up, yet the strain to his left side was more than noticeable. He was right, he told himself, to change his mind about saddling the black and riding out. It would have to wait one more day. But it would not wait longer. In the morning he would ride out. He took a deep drag on the smoke and filled his lungs.

Something wasn't right. There were some things that didn't fit together. He couldn't even tell himself what the things were, but he had a sense that inside his head there was a puzzle. All the pieces were there, but he couldn't fit them in place. It was an uneasy feeling, a stupid feeling, and he didn't like it. He threw away the cigarette, eased himself down off the fence, and walked back to the house. A cup of Agnes Lanagan's coffee would taste real good.

The next morning Colfax shaved and dressed, ate a hearty breakfast prepared by Agnes Lanagan, thanked her for all her kindness, and took his leave. He saddled the black mare without too much discomfort and rode to Pullman. It was a slow and easy ride. He knew better than to be overconfident. There was still pain in his side, but he managed to get to town without any problems. He left the mare in the hands of Jerry Slayton and went to the Railhead for coffee. There he found the actors. As soon as he walked in the door, Adrian Channing jumped up and rushed to greet him.

"Mr. Colfax," he said, "how good to see you about. Would you join us?"

"Thank you, Mr. Channing. I will."

Channing conducted Colfax to a table where Dixon Lindsay and Alma Dyer were seated.

"Good morning, ladies," said Colfax. "You're looking lovely this morning."

"Why, thank you, Mr. Colfax," said Alma.

"That's quite an accomplishment for us under the circumstances," said Dixon, "but then, our business is deception."

Colfax smiled as he took a seat.

"Yes," he said. "Do you mind if I smoke?"

"Not at all," said Dixon.

"Not if you allow me the same privilege," said Alma.

Colfax looked at Alma with mild surprise, then handed her the makings across the table.

"By all means," he said. He watched with a certain amount of admiration as the actress deftly rolled herself a cigarette, then handed the makings back to him. He took the tin matchbox out of his pocket and gave it to her, and she lit her smoke. Then Colfax rolled his own and lit it. The waiter came to the table, and Colfax ordered coffee.

"I take it there were no problems last night," said Colfax.

"No," said Channing. "Nothing. Of course, we were all a bit uneasy. None of us slept well, but nothing out of the ordinary transpired. We took your advice and stayed together—as much as possible. I spoke to the manager, and we consolidated our rooms. All the gentlemen are together in two rooms, and the ladies are in a room which is connected to one of ours. The one that I am in."

"Good." said Colfax.

"But how long must we keep this up?" asked Dixon.

"I hope not for much longer," said Colfax. "I'll do everything I can."

Alma Dyer reached out and put her hand on top of Colfax's hand, which was resting on the table. It seemed sudden to Colfax, almost shocking. And her touch sent waves of feeling up through his arm and into the rest of his body. He almost shuddered from the unexpected sensation.

"We know you will," she said, "and we appreciate what you're doing more than we can say."

Then she removed her hand, and he was sorry. He missed it there, missed the feeling. He flushed slightly, and he was afraid that the flush was visible. His face felt hot. He took a deep drag on his cigarette, leaned his head back, and expelled the smoke toward the ceiling.

"Mr. Channing," he said, "we have a little business together. Could we take care of that now?"

"What?" said Channing. "Oh. Oh, yes. Of course."

"Would you ladies excuse us for a few minutes?" said Colfax.

Channing took Colfax upstairs in the Railhead and unlocked the room in which he was staying. There were two interior doors in the room. Channing motioned to the door on his right.

"That leads to the ladies' room," he said. He walked to the other door and opened it. "Mr. Chase stays in here. Come on. Everyone else is downstairs with strict orders to remain together. We should have plenty of time."

Channing shuffled about the room until he found a particular traveling chest. He unlatched it and threw open the lid.

"This is his," he said. Colfax crossed the room quickly to join in the search. Among Chase's clothing and other personal belongings, they found two pairs of boots. Neither pair was the right style.

"That's strange," said Channing. "They should be here. I made a point of noticing what he had on today. He's wearing shoes. The cowboy boots should be here in his trunk."

"Maybe it's not so strange," said Colfax.

"What do you mean?"

"Mr. Channing," said Colfax, "if you had committed a murder and left a distinctive bloody boot print, what would you do?"

The old man's eyes opened wide, and he responded in a harsh whisper.

"Why, I'd get rid of the telltale boots, of course."

"Mr. Channing," said Colfax, "for now, let's keep this to ourselves. It isn't proof. There are other possible reasons for the boots to be missing. But keep a close eye on Mr. Chase, and be careful."

Chapter Thirteen

Colfax and Channing had just gone outside when Colfax noticed that a wagon loaded with the Wheelers, all of them, was pulling up in front of the general store. He angled his walk across the street in order to meet them.

"Hello, Mr. Colfax," said Dora Wheeler, as Colfax and Channing approached the wagon. "You look much better than when I last saw you."

"Thanks to you, Mrs. Wheeler," said Colfax. "This is Mr. Adrian Channing. I believe all of you saw him on the stage."

"How do you do, Mr. Channing?" said Dora.

"This is Lark Wheeler," said Colfax. "His lovely wife, Dora, and his brothers, Spud and Tommy."

"It's a pleasure to meet all of you," said Channing.

Lark, who was busy securing his team to the hitch rail, said, "Howdy." Spud nodded his head a bit grudgingly. Tommy sat in the back of the wagon, his head down. Colfax thought that he looked like a pouting child. He wondered what was wrong with the young man. Usually he was smiling and friendly. Maybe he had done something to make one of his brothers fuss at him, and it had put him in a sour mood. Tommy's cuts and bruises were beginning to fade, but his scuffed-up face still added to the appearance of a bad boy. Colfax reached over the wagon box and slapped Tommy on the shoulder.

"What's the matter here?" he said. "You all right?"

"Yeah," said Tommy. "I guess so."

Colfax thought that Tommy was glaring at Adrian Channing. Oh, well, he thought, who knows what goes on in the mind of a child, and that's what Tommy's got, it seems—a child's mind.

"In town for your shopping, I suppose?" said Channing, more to break the silence than for any other reason.

"Yes," said Dora.

"That and to stay as far away from the fireworks as we can," grumbled Spud.

Colfax shot Spud a quick look.

"Fireworks?" he said. "What are you talking about?"

Spud looked away, but Lark walked over to face Colfax.

"You don't know?" he asked.

"What fireworks?" said Colfax.

"Tiff Lanagan and his whole crew rode up to Youngblood's. They're up there now, waiting."

"Damn," said Colfax. "Come on, Channing. I've got to get the sheriff."

"Don't waste your time," said Lark. "He rode up with them."

"Well," Colfax said, "that's something. At least he took the law with him. That's more sense than I gave him credit for. I still think I ought to go up there. Mr. Wheeler, any sign of Youngblood coming back?"

"Not by the time we left the house."

"Thanks," said Colfax. "Channing, I'm taking you back to your people, and then I'm going to have to leave town for a while. Just keep doing as I told you. Keep everyone together at all times. Be careful. I'll get back as soon as I can."

Colfax caught himself pushing the black too hard in his haste to get up the mountain to the camp of Youngblood and his gang of rustlers. He forced himself to ease off some, to establish a sensible pace. Dort was up there with Lanagan and his crew. That was some small comfort. Colfax had almost no respect for Dort, but the man did represent the law. The fact that Lanagan had taken him along must mean that Lanagan intended to do things right, to try to capture the rustlers and have them arrested and tried. Colfax was astonished at himself. *If anyone had told me back before I'd met Bluff Luton that I would be worrying about having things done according to the law, I'd have said that he was crazy. Well, hell, times change, and people change with them,* he thought. *One way or the other, this job will soon be over.* He could see on the trail going up the hill evidence that several men on horseback had passed by ahead of him not long ago. The problem was that he had no way of telling if what he saw was only the result of Lanagan's trip or if Youngblood's crew had also come back. He wanted to get there before the return of the rustlers. He wanted to be there to do what he could to make sure that the outlaws were arrested, were taken alive, if possible. There should be a trial, even if the end result was the same. He had found the evidence. He had pointed Lanagan to the Youngbloods. If Lanagan and his cowboys should slaughter the rustlers, he would have helped them to do it.

It was midafternoon. Back in Pullman, in the restaurant inside the Railhead, the actors still huddled together. Samuel Chase was drinking rum rather heavily. All were bored and irritable. Chase had obviously just had harsh words with the other actors seated at the table with him. He stood up, bottle in one hand and glass in the other.

"Shit," he said, and he walked away from the table. Adrian Channing, in a fatherly attempt to try to raise the spirits of his children, had left the two ladies alone at their table and was mingling with others around the room, moving from one table to the next and cracking jokes. Chase saw the two women sitting alone and made his weaving way to their table.

"May I join you ladies?" he said, but he didn't wait for an answer. He set his bottle and glass down on the table and pulled out a chair, then dropped himself heavily into it and leaned over close to Dixon Lindsay.

"Mrs. Lindsay," he said, in an exaggerated theatrical voice. He had something more to say, but Dixon Lindsay didn't allow it. She pushed her chair back quickly from the table and stood up, shouting at the same time.

"Get away from me," she said. "Get away."

"What the hell?" said Chase.

"Get out."

Dixon appeared to be on the verge of hysteria. Alma Dyer got up and moved hurriedly to her side, putting an arm around her shoulders.

"Dixon," she said. "Calm down. What's the matter with you?"

Everyone in the room was looking at the woman and Chase. Some got to their feet. Channing ran across the room to deal with the problem.

"You know what's the matter," Dixon said to Alma. "You were there. He's the murderer."

"What the bloody hell is she talking about?" said Chase.

"Damn it, Dixon," said Channing. "Colfax told us to keep this to ourselves. We agreed."

"I can't help it," she said. "I've had as much of this as I can take."

C. C. Carpenter, the Bassianus of the play, a powerfully built man with a booming voice, stepped forward.

"I don't know what the hell this is all about," he said, "but I think that someone had better tell us."

"But there's no proof of anything," said Channing. "Only speculation."

"We're all in this together," said Carpenter. "We're waiting."

Channing looked around and found himself totally surrounded by his own acting company. As he looked, they moved in a little closer. The only ones not included in the group that pressed him were himself and Chase, who was still seated at the table. Suddenly Channing's players seemed to him to be a very threatening group, almost a mob. Beads of sweat formed on the old man's brow as his eyes shifted from one familiar face to another. He pulled a handkerchief out of his pocket and mopped his brow.

"All right," he said finally. "I suppose there's no getting away from it now, is there? The cat's out of the bag, so to speak. Well, uh, everyone sit down and I'll tell it all."

He waited while the company did as he said. Then he found himself facing a small and hostile crowd, with Samuel Chase sitting alone off to his right.

"Now mind you, children," he said, "this is a theory. One of several, as a matter of fact. As I think you all know, Mr. Oliver Colfax has taken a personal interest in our problems. When poor Dallas was murdered, Mr. Colfax determined to help track down the guilty party. I've had several conversations with Mr. Colfax during the course of his investigation. Initially we thought Dallas had been killed because of his color. That is, we thought the killer had done the deed because of the color of Dallas's skin. But then the killer struck again. This time the victims, as you know, were Woody and Tyndall. Three actors had been murdered. It seemed then that all of us might be in danger, that some maniac was bent on ridding society of actors."

Channing paused to catch his breath, gather his wits, and mop his brow again. He was struck by the frightening, deadly silence in the room in the absence of his own voice. The silence was suddenly broken by the sound of approaching footsteps, and Channing looked over his shoulder to see the waiter coming in his direction. He waved the man away.

"No. No," he shouted. "Not now, please."

He looked over his audience once again, then took a deep breath.

"To continue," he said, "a second theory was put forth. If the killings were not the work of a madman, then the only explanation seemed to be that the killer must have known all of the victims. As Mr. Colfax pointed out to me, the only people in Pullman who know all of us are—us."

"So the killer must be one of us?" said Carpenter.

"Well, yes. If that theory is the correct one."

"So why point the finger at me?" said Chase.

"You hated Dallas," said Dixon. "We've all heard you call him an uppity nigger."

Samuel Chase paled and poured himself another drink.

"Well," he said, "what about Woody and Tyndall? I never had anything against them. They were friends of mine."

"What about it, Adrian?" said Carpenter.

"The theory is—that Sammy might have murdered Dallas for the reasons just alluded to. Then perhaps Woody and Tyndall, having heard, seen, or surmised something, became threats to Sammy. To avoid exposure, he had to murder them as well."

"It makes sense," said Dixon.

"But where's the proof?" said Carpenter. "Like Adrian said, it's only a theory."

"There is one other—small matter," said Channing.

"Well, go ahead," said Dixon. "Tell them."

"Dallas Potter's murderer left behind a bloody boot print. The boot was a cowboy boot with a slashed right sole—about a size seven or eight.

"That's not very exact," said Chase. "So I wear a size seven and a half. If you take all the sevens, seven-and-a-halfs, and eights, that's a lot of suspects."

"We've all seen you in cowboy boots," said Dixon.

"It seems to me," said Carpenter, "that we could resolve this rather easily by checking the sole of Sammy's right boot."

"Mr. Colfax and I attempted to do that," said Channing, "and the boots were nowhere to be found."

"Of course not," said Chase. "I threw them away. They pinched my feet."

Carpenter stood up and took a step toward Chase. He folded his arms across his chest and looked down at his fellow actor.

"Where are they, Sammy?" he asked. "Where did you toss them?"

"I tossed them while we were down in New Mexico."

"The boots would have proved his guilt," said Dixon, "so naturally he got rid of them. How much more do we have to hear? He's the killer."

"I think that one of us had better go for the sheriff," said Carpenter.

"No," said Chase.

"The sheriff is out of town, I'm afraid," said Channing, "on a rustler hunt, I believe."

Chase lurched to his feet, bumping into the edge of the tabletop and knocking over his bottle. Rum ran across the tabletop and onto the floor.

"You can't believe this," he said. "This is insane. You all know me."

"There's a deputy or something, isn't there?" asked Carpenter.

"Yes," said Channing. "I believe so."

Carpenter turned to leave the room, presumably to follow his own advice and seek out the law, but when his back was turned to Chase, Chase reached out and grabbed him by the shoulders.

"No, you won't," he shouted, and he jerked Carpenter by the shoulders, flinging him backward to the floor. Then he started to run toward the door, but Dixon was in his path. He swept her aside with his left arm, only to find his path again blocked. This time it was Adrian Channing who had stepped up deliberately to stop Chase. He put his two large hands out in front of himself and shoved, giving Chase a hard bump on the chest and sending him backward a couple of steps. By then, Carpenter was back on his feet, and as Chase staggered backward, Carpenter wrapped both his arms around him from behind. Chase struggled, but Carpenter's powerful bear hug was more than he could take. He finally gave up and let his body hang limp in the big man's grasp.

"One of you men run down to the sheriff's office and bring the deputy," said Channing.

Chase was panting heavily. Finally he caught his breath long enough to speak.

"I didn't do it," he said. "I didn't do anything."

Chapter Fourteen

Samuel Chase was manhandled down the street and into the jail, where Haskell Gibbs, after hearing the case against him, locked him in a cell. Chase shouted out his innocence through the bars.

"Well," said Gibbs, "I ain't going to charge you with nothing. I'll just hold you here until the sheriff gets back, and then he can decide what to do with you."

"Then what the hell are you holding me for?"

Gibbs scratched his head, a perplexed expression on his face.

"Questioning," he said finally.

Chase grabbed the bars with both hands and pressed his face into them.

"Adrian," he shouted. "Adrian, get me out of here."

"I—I can't, Sammy," said Channing. "Not just yet, anyway. We'll have to get this whole thing cleared up. I'm sorry."

The old man was looking at the floor rather than at Chase.

"You know I didn't kill anyone, Adrian. Adrian, you know me."

"Sammy," said Channing, "I just don't know. I wouldn't have

thought so, but it—it's all so horrible. I just don't know what to think. I'll talk to Mr. Colfax as soon as he returns."

Channing turned and walked out of the jail. Just as he pulled the door shut behind himself, Chase shouted after him.

"You talk to the sheriff and get me out of here."

Outside, a small group of Pullman's citizens had gathered on the sidewalk in front of the jail. As Channing stepped out, one of them put a hand on his shoulder.

"What's going on in there?" he said. "Is that the killer in there?"

"We don't know," said Channing. "He's being held for questioning. That's all."

The citizen turned away from Channing to address his friends.

"Damn, boys," he said. "They've got that murderer in there."

"There's been nothing proved yet," said Channing. "He's only being held for questioning."

But the citizens had already lost interest in Channing, and they ignored him completely.

Youngblood and Hughes rode along side by side on the trail which ran alongside the river. They had passed the Wheelers' home several miles back and would soon be at their camp. Behind them rode the three remaining members of the band of rustlers. They rode easy. It had been a long and hard ride, and they knew better than to push their mounts, even this close to home. They had gotten rid of the stolen cattle that would have incriminated them, and they had money in their pockets. They felt good.

"We'll just lay low for a while, Youngblood," Hughes was saying. "Take it easy. If we take off out of here, Colfax will surely put it all together and come after us. But he won't do anything without evidence. He's dead set that way. I'll keep riding along with him until he gets tired of this game and decides to fire me. You and the boys just stay put up here. Go ahead and pick up some strays now and then. We'll just wait him out."

"Why don't we just kill him and have it done with?" said Youngblood.

"That would set off Lanagan for sure. No, we'll wait it out. At least for a while."

"You're the boss," said Youngblood, but his tone indicated that he wasn't particularly happy with the plan.

Hughes turned in his saddle to look at the riders coming up behind him.

"Jonsey," he said, "is that stuff in your saddlebags safe?"

"Hell, yes, Rondo," said the man addressed as Jonsey. "Ain't no way I'm going to let a bottle of good whiskey get broke."

"Just a few more minutes," said Hughes, "and we'll be passing it around."

Billy O. had discovered the same rock perch overlooking the trail from which Denny Doyle had fired upon Colfax and Hughes a few days earlier. He saw Hughes and Youngblood round a curve in the trail below and, immediately after, the three other riders. He scampered down off the rock, jumped into his saddle, and raced back to the Youngblood camp.

"They're coming, Mr. Lanagan," he said.

"Get your horse out of sight," ordered Lanagan. The other horses had already been hidden away. Billy O. hurried to hide his, as Lanagan turned to Boyd Gruver to issue further orders. "Get everyone into position, Boyd," he said. "Now."

Gruver shouted a few quick commands and punctuated them with directional gestures. Cowboys hustled around the camp, moving into the tents, behind rocks and trees, some on one side of the river, some on the other. Tiff Lanagan and Sheriff Dort sat side by side on a log by the ashes where the fire had burned itself out. They waited.

Back in Pullman, the Wheeler brothers had left Dora to do some shopping, agreeing to meet her at a specified place and time later in the day. They had just walked out onto the sidewalk when they saw the mob approaching the jail. There were at least a dozen men in the unruly group, all shouting at once. In the lead was a man the Wheelers recognized from their infrequent visits to town. His name was MacGowan, and he was carrying a rope. Some of the men in the mob still had bottles in their hands. They had apparently worked themselves up to do their civic duty in one of the local saloons.

"Damn," said Lark Wheeler. "I ain't never seen one before, but if that ain't a lynch mob, I'll ride naked down main street at high noon."

"That's a pretty safe bet," said Spud. "They ain't going to no tea party."

"What?" said Tommy. His eyes opened wide in horror. "Those men? What are they going to do?"

"They're going to drag that actor out of jail and hang him," said Spud.

"How come?"

"They think he killed them other actors."

"They're drunk," said Lark.

"They shouldn't do that," said Tommy. "Should they? That's bad, ain't it?"

"Well," said Lark with a heavy sigh, "it ain't legal and proper. They ought to have a trial first, at least."

Tommy turned and started to hurry away.

"Where are you going?" said Lark.

"I'm going away from here. I don't want to see them."

"Well, don't go far," said Lark. "You know where to meet us?"

"I know."

"And when?"

"I know," said Tommy, and he ran down to the corner and disappeared around the edge of the building.

"Tommy's right for once," said Lark.

"About what?"

"They shouldn't be doing that. The man ain't even had a trial. They don't know if he done the killings or not."

"Well, it ain't our worry," said Spud, but the expression on his face belied his statement of unconcern. "Let's go get a drink."

"Sheriff's out of town," said Lark, ignoring his brother's suggestion. "So's Colfax."

"They picked a good time, all right," said Spud. "They ain't too drunk for that."

The mob had reached the door to the sheriff's office and jail and found it locked. Someone was rattling the door. The shouting was louder than before.

"Break it down," someone shouted.

"Someone ought to do something," said Lark.

"Let it go," said Spud. "He's probably guilty anyhow. It won't make no difference to him whether they hang him with or without a trial."

"Well, I ain't going to just stand here," said Lark, and he headed for the jail.

"Lark," shouted Spud. "Damn it."

Lark was about in the middle of the street when Spud turned and ran toward where the Wheeler wagon stood waiting, but once Lark started moving, he didn't look back. He had no idea what Spud might be up to. He rushed up to the mob and fought off an impulse to smash right into them. Lark stopped in the street just behind them, pulled his Remington Army .44 out of his waistband, and fired a shot into the wall of the sheriff's office above the heads of the mob. The shouts stopped, and the mob turned slowly to face Lark. From his position up close to the door, MacGowan pushed his way through the crowd.

"Lark Wheeler," he said. "What's your interest in this?"

"I just don't like what you're doing here, MacGowan. Why don't you all just wait for the sheriff to get back?"

"We done talked all that over, Wheeler," said MacGowan. "Put your gun away and walk off, and we'll just forget about what you done here. We got no quarrel with you."

"You do if you try to hang that man in there without a trial."

"Without a trial? Hell, what's a trial? They get twelve men together to decide whether or not a man's guilty. Right? There's twelve of us right here, and we decided. He's guilty, and we're going to hang him."

Lark deliberately aimed his revolver at MacGowan's chest and pulled back the hammer for a second shot.

"Not if I can stop you," he said.

MacGowan kept his eyes on Lark, but spoke to the eleven men behind him.

"Spread out, boys," he said. The mob on the sidewalk began to move, and soon it was no longer a mob but a long line of men. Lark had to shift his eyes back and forth even to see from one end of the line to the other. MacGowan watched Lark's eyes flit back and forth a time or two, and he grinned.

"You can't take us all," he said. "Give it up."

"I'll take you down," said Lark. "You first."

MacGowan held his hands out to his sides, palms open toward Lark. He moved his fingers in a beckoning gesture. His eyes stayed on Lark.

"Come on down, boys," he said. "Slow and easy."

The ends of the long line eased down into the street, and it began to form itself into a horseshoe shape around Lark. Lark turned from one end of the line to the other.

"Hold it," he shouted. "Back up."

"You just got four shots, Wheeler," said MacGowan. "You use one of them to kill me, these boys'll be all over you. They'll hang you first and get the actor next."

Lark felt a sense of panic developing deep down in his gut. MacGowan was right. He had four shots left. He only loaded five for reasons of safety, keeping the hammer on an empty chamber, and he had fired one over the heads of the mob. He was beginning to feel like a damn fool for taking on a mob with nothing but a revolver. Spud had told him to leave it alone. He should have listened. He could still put down the weapon and back off. They would let him go if he did. But he couldn't bring himself to do that. He couldn't shoot MacGowan while the man was just standing there, not making any move toward him, but if he didn't do something soon, the horseshoe would become a circle and enclose him. Then they would get him from behind. MacGowan grinned again.

"You don't have a chance against us," he said.

"But I do."

MacGowan looked toward his right over the heads of his cohorts to see Spud Wheeler standing in the street, a long-barreled shotgun aimed generally at the mob. When Spud had seen his brother make his initial move toward the jail, he had run for the Wheeler wagon to get the shotgun out from under the seat. It was a Remington 10-gauge with two twenty-eight-inch barrels.

"They're both loaded," said Spud. "Both cocked. I can probably cut all of you in half."

Chapter Fifteen

Colfax had estimated that he was about a half mile below the Wheelers' place when he noticed the black begin to favor her right foreleg. He eased up on her, but continued to move ahead. In a few more steps, she had developed a decided limp, and Colfax stopped her and dismounted. He moved around to her right side and lifted the leg.

"Damn," he said, following a brief examination of the sole of her hoof, "stone bruise. Hell, I can't ride you up this hill like that, old girl. Come on. Let's walk."

He took the reins in his left hand and started walking up the trail. He hoped that his estimate of the distance to Wheeler's place was at least close to correct. He sure didn't want to walk more than half a mile, and he was in a hurry. Some things just can't be hurried, though, he thought. He recalled that the Wheelers had gone to town in a wagon. Their saddle horses should be in the corral then. He would leave the black there in the corral to be dealt with later and borrow one of Wheeler's mounts to get on up to Youngblood's camp. Or should he call it Hughes's camp?

Damn that Rondo Hughes. From the beginning, he had thought that Rondo might possibly be mixed up with Youngblood, but he had decided not to judge the man prematurely. He had thought that it was just as likely that Rondo was telling the truth about himself. He had hired Rondo in order to help himself resolve the question. If Rondo was straight, then he would be some help to Colfax. If Rondo was crooked, he would eventually reveal himself and probably the other rustlers. It was the second possibility that had eventually proved to be true, but Colfax didn't like it. He had developed a kind of fondness for Rondo Hughes. *Damn,* he thought, *there was a time when I'd have thought the worst about Rondo or about any other man. Sarge has ruined me for this kind of work. Sure as hell, it's quitting time.*

Wheeler's corral didn't have a real gate, just a couple of rails laid across the opening in the fence. When he reached the corral, Colfax tossed the rails down and led the black inside the enclosure. He replaced the top rail and unsaddled the black, then gave her a couple of pats.

"Someone will be along and tend to you real soon," he said.

He turned to look over the horses in the corral. He had been right. There were three cow ponies milling around. They seemed just a bit nervous at the intrusion of a stranger into their midst. He intended to take the bridle and bit off of the black and put it on one of Wheeler's horses, but out of the corner of his eye he noticed a hackamore lying in the dirt beside the fence on the back side of the corral. It had probably been thrown across the top rail of the fence carelessly and had fallen to the ground. Colfax moved over to the spot where the hackamore lay and bent to pick it up, and there beside it in the dirt something else caught his attention. He knelt in the dirt to inspect it more closely, to be sure.

"Damn," he said in a barely audible whisper.

It was a clear boot print. It was small, right-footed, and it had a slash across the sole.

Haskell Gibbs was standing at the bar inside the Railhead. He was putting down his third glass of whiskey. Adrian Channing was at the front window, nervously watching the action at the jail. It appeared to be a standoff between the mob and the two men who had moved to stop them.

"Deputy," he said, "you've got to go over there and help those two men."

Gibbs took another swallow of whiskey.

"Deputy. Damn you, it's your job."

"I ain't going to get myself killed for no throat-cutting murderer," said Gibbs. "Just leave me alone."

Channing turned back to the window in disgust and despair, and Gibbs tipped his glass for another slurp, just as a high-pitched and horrified scream ripped through the silence. Gibbs dropped his glass. Channing turned and ran toward the lobby of the hotel. Behind the front desk a startled Monroe Bates gestured wildly as he saw Channing.

"Upstairs," he said.

Channing took the stairs two at a time, and as he reached the landing at the top, Alma Dyer ran hysterically into his arms. He clutched her to him, looking wildly over her shoulder.

"What?" he said. "What is it?"

"In my room," said Alma. "Oh, God. It's Dixon."

Gibbs stood halfway up the stairs, weaving slightly, and watched as Channing moved down the hallway toward the room.

Youngblood saw the two men sitting on the log by the dead ashes. Even when he recognized them, he kept moving slowly into the camp. He didn't call a halt until he was close, just across the ashes from Lanagan and Dort. The two men still sat on the log, but they were looking at Youngblood and his crew.

"You're pretty brave, old man," said Youngblood. "You and your pet lawman. Coming up here like this all alone."

"Not alone," said Lanagan. "Step out, boys."

Armed cowboys emerged from their hiding places all over the camp. All held guns pointed at the five rustlers.

"We've got you dead to rights this time," said Dort. "Drop your guns and climb down out of them saddles."

"And then what?" said Rondo Hughes.

"No," shouted Youngblood, reaching for his six-gun. From his spot beside a tree, Boyd Gruver fired a Henry .44 rifle. The shot hit Youngblood in the sternum knocking him out of the saddle. Hughes made a dive off his horse and ran toward the trees, but a shot tore through the back of his knee, smashing the kneecap as it exited. He roared in pain and fell to the ground rolling, just as Jonsey pulled his revolver out and sent a shot tearing into the left biceps of Billy O. Link, standing in the doorway to the tent just behind Lanagan and Dort, raised a rifle and fired. The bullet smashed into Jonsey's forehead, causing his head to jerk backward. Then it slumped forward, and Jonsey's body sagged lifeless in the saddle. The two remaining rustlers lashed their mounts and headed into the river crossing. Halfway across, they were knocked from their saddles by a hail of bullets from the guns of several cowboys in the camp. Sheriff Dort walked over to where Rondo Hughes lay. Hughes had dropped his Colt when he fell. He was reaching out for it when Dort stepped on his hand. Suddenly there was silence, and then the lifeless body of Jonsey slipped from the saddle and fell to the ground with a dull thud.

Colfax had managed to tear his attention away from the telltale boot print in the Wheelers' corral to get the hackamore on one of the Wheeler horses. As important as the boot print was, there was something about to happen up ahead that was more urgent. He had gotten the horse saddled and out of the corral and had replaced the rails that served as a gate, when he heard the shots. Damn, he thought. He was too late. He kicked his heels into the horse's sides and lashed at it with the long ends of the reins. It sounded like a small war up ahead, and Colfax knew that he would be a fool to race headlong into something like that, yet he felt a desperation to get there, to try to stop it. He wasn't sure why. The ride seemed longer than it had before, in spite of the fact that Colfax was riding it much faster than he had before. He hadn't gone far when the shots had ceased. He knew it was over. Yet he continued to race up the trail.

When he reached the camp, two cowboys were dragging two bodies out of the river. Two more bodies, one he recognized as that of Youngblood, were lying near the cold ashes of what had been the campfire. Link was tying a red bandanna around the bloody left biceps of Billy O., and Boyd Gruver, on horseback, was slipping a noose over the head of Rondo Hughes, who was mounted, his hands tied behind his back, blood running freely from a wound in his knee. Sheriff Dort was standing behind the horse on which Hughes was mounted.

"God," said Colfax, and he urged his borrowed horse toward the group beneath the hanging tree. Lanagan stepped toward him.

"It's over, Colfax," he said. "Go on back down to the ranch. You'll get your pay."

Colfax rode past Lanagan, moving with more urgency, and Rondo Hughes saw him coming.

"Colfax," shouted Hughes, his voice a desperate plea. Dort slapped the horse hard across the rump, causing the surprised animal to lunge forward carrying Rondo along with it until the slack was gone from the rope. Hughes was jerked out of the saddle, his feet well forward and high off the ground. Colfax heard the awful choking sound that escaped from Hughes's throat, saw the body swing gracefully and grotesquely backward, watched as its arcs grew shorter and shorter, saw it spin simultaneously with the swinging, witnessed the changing expressions and complexion on the painfully contorted and horrified face as the life was slowly choked out of Rondo Hughes.

Colfax felt a sudden dull revulsion welling up from the depths of his guts, as if in the very bottom of his stomach there was a small, stale pool of water stagnating, its fetid fumes rising and bringing into his mouth a bitter taste of bile. He felt like there was something in there he would like to vomit forth in order to cleanse himself of its taint. But he had no physical urge to retch, so the unwelcome intruder in his body continued to lie there and fester.

Lanagan walked up to stand beside Colfax, who still sat on the back of the horse from Wheeler's corral. Both men stared at what had been Rondo Hughes, still spinning and swinging ever so slightly.

"You didn't even break his damn neck," said Colfax.

"That's too bad," said Lanagan, and the irony was that he sounded as if he meant it. "We didn't have time to build a scaffold."

Maybe Lanagan was right. The end would have been the same. There was no doubt of that. Where had Colfax developed this need for propriety? What difference would a trial have made? Colfax knew that if he had been there, the gunfight would have occurred, probably just about the same way. The rustlers would have resisted, and he would have helped to kill them. That part he could easily understand. But the hanging—he wouldn't have done that, wouldn't have allowed it to be done. He'd have taken Hughes down to Pullman and put him in jail. There would have been a trial. It would have been handled—properly.

"Your black horse is down in Wheeler's corral," he said, not looking at Lanagan as he spoke. "She's got a stone bruise. You can have one of your cowboys pick her up and tend to her. I'll stop by your ranch later to get my pay." He rode down the hill back to Wheeler's place and put the borrowed horse back in the corral. Then he started walking toward Pullman.

Haskell Gibbs tried to strut as he headed for the mob outside of the jail, but he had poured too much whiskey down his throat to manage it effectively. He staggered and swayed, but he did manage to get himself there. Spud Wheeler still held his shotgun leveled at the mob. Lark still stood with his revolver in hand, pointed at the chest of MacGowan. The mob still stood in a horseshoe shape half surrounding Lark. No one was speaking as Gibbs stepped into the horseshoe.

"You can all put your guns away and go on home," said Gibbs. "There's been another killing. That man in there ain't guilty. I'm turning him loose."

"Another killing," said MacGowan. "When?"

"Just now. Well, anyhow, since we put him in there. He couldn't have done it."

Lark lowered his revolver, eased the hammer down, and tucked it back into his waistband. Taking his cue from his older brother, Spud eased down the hammers of the long shotgun and lowered it.

"Who's been killed?" asked someone in the crowd.

"One of them actresses," said Gibbs. "Her throat's cut."

Lark turned to his brother. His face was grim. He took Spud by the arm and started to walk away from the crowd.

"Where the hell's Tommy?" he said.

"Gibbs," said MacGowan, "that's four killings in our town. You got any idea who's responsible for them?"

"Not a clue," said Gibbs.

"Well, you're the law. You better damn well get to the bottom of this. We pay you to protect us here."

"You all got any complaints," said Gibbs, "you take them to Sheriff Dort. He's my boss. He's in charge. I ain't. All I do is just what the sheriff tells me to do."

"Well, where the hell is Dort?" said MacGowan.

"He's out taking care of rustlers right now. He'll be back in here soon. You can take all this up with him when he gets back."

Chapter Sixteen

Colfax was limping when he walked into the Railhead. He stopped at the desk where Monroe Bates was on duty.

"Mr. Bates," he said, "I want you to close out the account for Tiff Lanagan right now. My job for him is finished. I'll pay the bill from here on."

"Yes, sir," said Bates.

"And have your man draw me a bath as quickly as possible."

Colfax made his way slowly up the stairs. It was dark out. He hadn't seen anyone as he walked into town. Nor had he seen anyone in the lobby of the hotel other than Bates. Inside his room, he left the door opened, sat on the edge of the bed, and pulled his boots off. Then he took off his hat and tossed it toward the table which stood to one side of the door. He missed, and it fell to the floor. He sat for a moment, staring across the room. Then he got up and pulled off his jacket, then his shirt. He felt old, old and tired and just a little sad.

"What a piece of work is man," he said to himself in a low voice.

He wanted a drink of good brandy. No. He wanted a bottle. He wanted to get drunk and to pass out and to drift away into oblivion—at least for a while. Then he remembered the boot print in Wheeler's corral and his promise to find the murderer of the actors. He had sworn off the booze until the job was done. Well, one job was done, but the other remained. The brandy would have to wait. When the bath was finally prepared, he shut and locked the door, then undressed and lowered himself into the hot water. Soon he was asleep.

Colfax surprised himself by waking up early the next morning. His feet were still tender from the long walk down the mountain trail, but otherwise he felt much better than he had the night before. He dressed and went downstairs for breakfast. As he moved to find himself a table, he saw Adrian Channing stand up and motion to him. He walked over to where Channing was at a table with Alma Dyer.

"Would you like to join us, Mr. Colfax?" said Channing.

Colfax looked down at Alma and took off his hat.

"With the lady's permission," he said. "It would be a pleasure."

"Please do," said Alma.

Colfax and Channing sat down.

"Mr. Colfax," said Channing, "while you were out yesterday, a terrible thing happened."

"Not—" Colfax began, but he was interrupted by Channing.

"Another murder," said the old man.

"My God," said Colfax. "Who?"

"Mrs. Lindsay," said Channing. "Dixon Lindsay."

"It was awful," said Alma. "I found her in our room."

"Oh, no," said Colfax. He put his head in his hand, his elbow on the table. "How—may I ask?"

"Her throat had been cut," said Channing.

"And Mr. Chase?"

"Was in jail. He couldn't possible have done it."

"I didn't think so," said Colfax. "I found a boot print made by the boot we're looking for. It was in a place Mr. Chase would not likely have been. But what was Chase doing in jail, and why was Mrs. Lindsay allowed to be alone?"

Channing told Colfax about the session among the actors that had led to the arrest of Chase, how it had been Dixon Lindsay who had let it out that Chase was suspected. He also told him about the would-be lynch mob and the Wheelers and how, if Alma Dyer had not discovered the body just when she did, there would likely have been more killings in Pullman that day.

"Dixon was sure that Sammy was the guilty party," said Alma, "so once he was locked up in jail, she felt safe. What with the murders and then the incident with Sammy, I'm afraid that we all were a bit testy. We were sniping at each other, and Dixon got rather nasty. She got up and left in a huff to go to the room. I should have gone with her. I thought of what you had said as she was leaving, but I suppose I was too angry at her at the moment to care. That's an awful thing to have to admit. Anyway, I let her go."

"Don't blame yourself," said Colfax.

The waiter appeared and asked what he could bring Colfax. Channing and Alma had already had their breakfast and coffee. Colfax was hungry, but with the news he had just received, he didn't really feel like eating—not just yet.

"Just coffee for now," he said. "Refills for these two."

As the waiter walked away, Channing leaned across the table toward Colfax and spoke in a low, confidential voice.

"Do you have any new ideas on this business?" he asked.

"No," said Colfax. "I'm afraid not, but I do have a new clue to follow up. I intend to pursue that today."

"The boot print?"

"Yes."

"Can you tell us where you found it?"

Colfax thought about the slipup with Chase and the more fatal one with Dixon Lindsay.

"It was up on the mountain," he said. "Away from town. I hope I'll know more this evening."

What Colfax wanted to do would be touchy. He wanted to go back to the Wheeler place and look around. He wanted to look for more bootprints and anything else he might find that would relate to the man who wore the boot. He couldn't just go to the Wheelers' home and start nosing around. They would want to know what he was up to. He wished that he had taken the time while he was there and they were still in town, but he had been in a hurry to get to Youngblood's on the way up the hill, and on his way back down his thoughts had been occupied with what he had seen at the camp. Well, he thought, he would just go up there and tell Lark Wheeler what he had seen, ask him if any strangers had been around who might have left the print, and ask him if he could look around. The Wheelers surely had nothing to fear from such an investigation.

Colfax drank two cups of coffee and decided that he should go ahead and eat. He didn't really feel like it, but he knew that he would need the energy before the day was up. He ordered a breakfast and ate it.

"Mr. Colfax," said Alma, as Colfax was getting up to leave, "are you going back up the mountain to look for more— evidence?"

"Yes, I am."

"Could I ride along with you?"

"Well," said Colfax, "I don't—"

"I'm going crazy in this town. I'd really like to get out. I can ride a horse."

"Mrs. Dyer," said Colfax, "I'm not sure what I'll find up there. I don't want to take you into any possible danger. But I don't suppose there's any great hurry for me to get up there this morning. Why don't we take a ride together right now. I'll go up the mountain after we get back."

They rode out of town toward the mountains alongside the river. Soon they were on range either owned or used—Colfax wasn't sure which—by Dierks. The terrain was still flat, but it was getting more rocky. Colfax stopped beside an outcropping of boulders on the bank of the river. They dismounted and walked to the water's edge. Alma Dyer sat on a boulder facing the river.

"It's beautiful here," she said. "I'll carry mixed memories of this country around with me the rest of my life."

"Yes," said Colfax. "I imagine you will."

He walked over to stand beside her. The water was rushing past them. He knew that it was cold, and he recalled the two bodies he had watched being dragged from this same river the day before up the mountain. He, too, he thought, would carry mixed memories of this country.

"Where will you go from here, Mr. Colfax?" asked Alma.

"I don't know. I have a friend. When I last saw him he was in Iowa. He was a town marshal there, but he was talking about going to Texas to a ranch. He said I would always be welcome. I may look him up."

"That sounds nice."

"What about you, Mrs. Dyer? What will you do?"

"It's Miss Dyer, really. Adrian thinks that it looks better on the tour to list the ladies as Mrs. But won't you call me Alma?"

"Thank you," said Colfax. "I will."

"And must I continue to call you Mr. Colfax?"

"Well, uh, I don't really fancy my first name. Sarge—that's my friend—he called me Cole. No one else ever did, but I guess that you could—call me Cole."

"I like that," said Alma. "I shall call you Cole."

"You didn't answer my question, Alma."

"Oh? What was it?"

"What will you do when this is all over?"

"I don't have anyplace to go but back to New York. I don't have anything to do but act. I suppose I'll go back and look for another job."

"You shouldn't have any problem there," said Colfax. "You're a fine actress."

"Thank you, but I'm afraid that my heart isn't in it anymore. Not the way it used to be. I wish—"

She paused and stared at the river rushing past. Colfax looked at her and waited for her to finish her wish. She didn't, and he sat down beside her.

"What do you wish, Alma?" he said.

"Oh, nothing," she said. "I'm being silly."

Colfax reached into his pocket for tobacco and papers. He started to roll a cigarette, paused, then held the makings out for Alma to look at.

"Do you mind?" he asked.

"Not at all."

He finished rolling his cigarette, lit it, and blew some smoke to the winds.

"Go ahead," he said.

"Go ahead what?"

"Be silly. I won't tell anyone."

"I don't even remember what I was saying," said Alma, and she laughed, a little musical laugh.

"You had started to express a wish."

"All right, then," she said. "I will. I wish that I could do like you. I wish I could say, I'm going to Texas, or something like that, and then do it. That's what I wish."

"You could give up your career?" said Colfax with surprise in his voice.

"I feel trapped in it, actually. It's a tiring life. The tours are especially exhausting. I've been working since I was seventeen years old, Cole. Yes. I'd like to be able to quit. And now these awful murders. Aaron and Chiron and Demetrius and now poor Tamora."

Colfax looked at Alma. His face registered a sudden realization. He started to speak but didn't. He knew. Now he knew. But he couldn't say it. Not yet. There was no proof. But the proof would be up on the hill. Damn, he thought. It was so simple. All it took to make everything clear was just what she said—the way she said it.

"Alma," he said, "do you believe that there are people so unsophisticated as to be unable to distinguish between the action on a stage and reality?"

"Oh, yes, of course there are. We don't encounter them so much in New York, but there are all kinds of tales about that sort of thing—well—out west. What are you getting at?"

"What kinds of tales?"

"Well, one I recall was that someone once shot the poor hound that was pursuing Eliza in a production of *Uncle Tom's Cabin.*"

"Really?"

"Yes."

"And do you think it was because he thought he was rescuing Eliza?"

"Well, I suppose there are other possibilities, but that's the way the story's always been told."

Colfax stood up from his seat on the rock. He took a final drag on his cigarette and tossed the butt away and paced off a few steps. Then he turned back to face Alma.

"And you believe it? I mean, you accept that the man killed the dog in an attempt to protect Eliza? He thought that what he was watching on the stage was real?"

"I don't really know, I suppose, but, yes, I think so. A child would think it was real, you know. Perhaps an adult with no experience of the theater would experience it for the first time rather like a child, wouldn't he?"

"Yes," said Colfax. "That's exactly it. Like a child."

Alma stood up and walked to Colfax. She put a hand on his arm. He looked troubled, and it worried her.

"Cole," she said, "what is it? What are you thinking?"

"You said it, Alma. Just now. You said Aaron and Chiron and Demetrius and Tamora. You know, when Mr. Potter was killed, I thought that it was because he was black. Then when the next two murders were committed, I thought it was someone out killing actors for some insane reason. I've been trying to figure out why anyone would want to kill actors—or why anyone would want to kill Potter, Granger, Tabor, and Mrs. Lindsay. You said Aaron, Chiron, Demetrius, and Tamora, and that's the key."

"What?"

"What do those four characters have in common?"

"Why—they are the tormentors of Lavinia, of course. I—oh, my God, Cole. Do you mean to say that they were all killed because—?"

"Because someone very unsophisticated and childlike saw them tormenting a lovely, innocent, helpless, young woman. I should have seen it, Alma. I should have figured it out sooner."

Colfax recalled the ashen-faced Tommy Wheeler as he was leaving the theater the night of the play. He remembered Tommy's new boots. Tommy's size was right. And, of course, the boot print in the corral.

"Cole," said Alma, a sudden desperation in her voice. "Cole, if you're right, we must hurry back to town. Adrian may be in terrible danger."

"Adrian?" said Colfax. "Damn, you're right. It was Titus himself who killed Lavinia."

Chapter Seventeen

Colfax banged the front door of the Railhead back against the wall in his haste as he rushed in, Alma Dyer right behind him. Passing by the front desk, he spoke brusquely to Monroe Bates.

"Is Mr. Channing in the lounge?"

"Yes, sir, I believe so, sir."

"Go get the sheriff and bring him back here. Quick."

Bates was out the front door about the same time Colfax went into the lounge with Alma still managing to keep up with him. Channing saw them as they stepped into the lounge, and he read the desperate intensity in their movements and expressions. He got up from his chair and hurried to meet them.

"What is it?" he said. "What's happening?"

"Thank God you're safe," said Alma.

Colfax looked around the room. There wasn't a large crowd, and they were mostly seated at tables up near the bar. He selected a corner table with no one near it, motioned toward it, and put a hand on the back of each of his companions.

"Let's take that table over there," he said, and he gave them each a gentle push in that direction. They walked across the room and sat down.

"For God's sake, Mr. Colfax," said Channing, "what's this all about?"

"Mr. Channing," said Colfax, "I know who the killer is, and I know that you are his next intended victim."

"What?"

"Now try to stay calm," said Colfax. "I'm going out to find him. In the meantime, I want you to stay here. Stay out in public with a crowd if possible. I've sent for the sheriff to be here while I'm gone."

"You know where to find this person?"

"I think so."

"Well, who is it, man?"

Colfax thought about what had happened in his absence when the word had gotten around that Chase was a suspect. He had said that he knew who the killer was, and he felt confident in that assertion. But there was always the possibility that he was wrong. And even if he was right, he didn't want an angry mob getting its hands on Tommy Wheeler. He had thought that when he found the murderer of these actors, he would have no mercy. He had thought that he would take delight in the killing of this deranged madman. But Tommy Wheeler was no madman. Tommy was a child in a man's body. Tommy was guilty of murder, but his guilt grew out of his innocence. It was the greatest irony Colfax had yet faced in his life. The murders of the four actors sickened him, but the thought of the fate of the poor, pitiful young man with the mind of a child filled him with indignation at the inequities of birth. Yet what if Tommy was not at home, not to be found? What if, while Colfax was up the hill searching, Tommy should make his way into Pullman to complete his convoluted sequence of justice? Channing had to be told.

"Mr. Channing," said Colfax, "please keep this to yourself. I don't want another mob incited to riot. I'm satisfied that I know who the killer is, but as before, I don't have proof. You remember young Tommy Wheeler?"

"Tommy Wheeler?" repeated Channing, his face wrinkled in a reflection of his mind's attempt to put a face with the name.

"The young man in the family we spoke to in the street," said Colfax. "They were in a wagon."

"Oh, yes. He seemed to be pouting, I believe. And he, uh, I thought he appeared to be a bit—slow."

"Yes," said Colfax with a sigh.

"I only saw him briefly," said Channing, "but I—oh, not him, surely."

"I'm afraid so, Mr. Channing," said Colfax. "He's the one. Tommy Wheeler. Perhaps Mrs. Dyer will explain it to you while I'm gone."

"Yes," said Alma.

Colfax glanced up and saw Dort coming in the door to the lounge. The lawman glanced around the room, spotted Colfax and Channing, and headed toward them.

"Be careful," Colfax said to Channing. He rose from his chair and put his hat on. "I'm going out after him now."

Colfax turned to leave just as Dort walked up.

"What's this all about, Colfax?" said Dort.

"Sheriff," said Colfax, "I don't have time to explain everything to you. I think I've identified the murderer, and I'm going after him. I sent for you to protect Mr. Channing here. He's next on the man's list."

Colfax turned and walked out of the lounge without another word.

"How the hell does he know that?" said Dort.

"Sheriff," said Alma Dyer, "if you'll sit down with us, I'll try to explain to you and Mr. Channing just how Mr. Colfax knows who the next target will be."

The saddle horses were gone from the Wheeler corral when Colfax arrived at the Wheeler place. The brothers, he figured, were out somewhere at work. Smoke was rising from the stove-pipe, so Dora Wheeler was inside, probably baking bread. Colfax felt somehow guilty. This was a happy family of good people.

For a fleeting moment, he thought of riding away. Then he remembered the savage slashing of Dallas Potter and the equally brutal knifings of Granger and Tabor, and he pictured the body of Dixon Lindsay with its throat slit. He steeled himself to his unpleasant task and recalled a line from *Hamlet*. "Cursed spite, that ever I was born to set it right." He urged his rented horse forward and halted it at the corral, where he dismounted and lapped the reins around the top rail. Then he ducked under the top rail and stepped over the bottom one to get inside the corral. The wagon team moved lazily away from him as he walked across the corral to the fence on the back side. The boot print was still there. It was still clear. It had been protected because it was almost under the fence rail. Any other individual prints in the corral had long since been trampled by the horses. Colfax studied the print for a long moment, as if he wished that it would vanish, or that it would somehow tell him that he had read it incorrectly. Finally he stood up and walked away from it. He looked around the corral for any others like it, but he found none.

He left the corral and started toward the house, but he stopped. What would he say to Dora Wheeler? He had no idea. How could he tell her what it was he was searching for? Facing Lark and Spud would be bad enough, but he didn't know how to face Dora. Again he thought of riding away, but just then Dora Wheeler opened the front door and stepped out of the house.

"Oh," she said. "Hello, Mr. Colfax. I thought I heard someone out here. How are you feeling?"

"I'm feeling just fine, Mrs. Wheeler," Colfax said. "Thanks to you."

"Well, what are you doing back up here? I thought that your— business up here was done."

"Mrs. Wheeler," said Colfax, "could I ask you where you throw your trash?"

"What? What for?"

"Please, Mrs. Wheeler."

"Well," she said, "it's right over here."

Dora Wheeler started walking around the far side of the house.

Colfax followed her. She led him behind the house and down a narrow trail a few yards back into the brush.

"Right here," she said, indicating a partially burned heap of trash. "Sometimes we burn it."

Colfax walked up close to the trash heap and squinted at it. He thought that he could see a worn piece of leather, but it was only slightly protruding out from under some discarded rags. He looked around, found a piece of branch about two and a half feet long, and picked it up. Then, probing with his stick, he uncovered the boots. They were not burned. He pulled them out of the trash pile with his stick and dropped them at his feet. He dropped the stick and squatted down to examine the boots. He picked up the right boot and turned it over. The sole had a slash across it. The boot still had traces of what Colfax figured must be the blood of Dallas Potter on the sole and in the slash. His elbows were on his knees, the boot in his left hand. He put his right hand to his forehead, took a deep breath, and sighed heavily.

"Mr. Colfax," said Dora, "what's this all about?"

Colfax stood up and faced Dora. He still held the boot in his left hand.

"This boot," he said, but he couldn't make the rest of the words come out. He heard the sound of approaching horses out on the trail in front of the house, and he felt a tremendous sense of relief. He glanced in the direction of the welcome noise.

"That'll be Lark and them," said Dora. She turned and walked back toward the house and around it to the riverside trail. Colfax followed. Lark and Spud were just dismounting in front of the house.

"Colfax?" said Lark. "What brings you up here?"

Colfax held the boot out for Lark to see.

"I just have one question for you, Mr. Wheeler," he said. "Did you know about this?"

Lark opened his mouth as if to speak, but he just stood there. Spud looked from Lark to Colfax in confusion. Suddenly he turned back to his horse and reached for the saddle gun there. Colfax had his Colt out and aimed at Spud before Spud had the rifle half-way out of its scabbard.

"Don't do that," he said.

"Let it go, Spud," said Lark.

"Damn it, Lark," said Spud. "You know what he's asking?"

"I know," said Lark. "I said let it go."

Spud turned loose of the rifle, and it slid back into the leather sheath. He turned slowly and took a couple of unsure steps back toward Colfax. Lark's hands went to his face and he started to sob.

"What is it, Lark?" said Dora. She got no answer, so she turned to Spud. "What is it? You better tell me what's going on."

Colfax shoved his Colt back into its holster, high and toward the front. Again he felt like he was the guilty party. Someone had to answer Dora's question, though.

"This boot," he said, "was worn by the man who murdered the actors."

"Tommy's boot?" said Dora. "Who would be wearing Tommy's boot? I—Oh, no. No. Lark?"

Lark took a deep breath and ceased his sobs. He wiped his eyes with one swipe of a sleeve, and drew himself up tall.

"You haven't answered my question," said Colfax.

"How can I answer it?" said Lark. "Did I know? Maybe I did, but I couldn't let myself believe it. No, I don't think I knew. Not really. Not until just now, seeing you there with that boot, hearing your question. I don't know how to answer your question, Colfax. God, he's my baby brother."

"All right," said Colfax. "We'll let that go. Where is he?"

"I thought he'd be here. He rode out with us this morning. A little while ago we couldn't find him. We thought that he'd probably gone home."

"He's got to be found," said Colfax. "He's got to be stopped."

"I know," said Lark. "I'm going with you."

Colfax wondered briefly about the advisability of riding after a killer alongside the man's brother, but he mentally shrugged off the worry and headed for his horse. This family was already hurting too much. Spud turned and started to swing into his saddle.

"You stay here, Spud," said Lark.

"He's my brother, too," said Spud.

"I don't want Dora here alone. Not now. Besides, Tommy might come back home. One of us needs to be here."

Spud took his horse by the reins and started walking him to the corral. Colfax and Lark headed down the trail.

Chapter Eighteen

The sun was nearly down when Tommy Wheeler reached Pullman. He tied his horse to a hitch rail on one of the side streets, then walked to the corner and peeked out onto the main street. He looked up and down. He saw some people walking along, but he didn't know them. He did not see the bad old man. He wondered how much time he would have before his brothers came looking for him. He hoped that he would be able to find the bad old man and do what he had to do and get back home before his brothers missed him. If they wanted to know where he had been, he would tell them that he had been at the river. He liked the river, and he spent a lot of time there. They would believe him if he said that he had been at the river. He wondered where the bad old man was. He walked down the street, the back street he had ridden in on, until he came to the back of the Railhead Hotel. He had seen the bad old man and the others who were with him go into the Railhead before. He might be in there. Lights were on already. It wasn't really dark yet. Not quite.

Tommy walked up close enough to look into one of the

lighted windows, but not so close that anyone inside would see him. He was looking into the kitchen. He saw the cooks and dishwashers rushing about, and he thought that they must have hard jobs. He was glad that he was a cowboy and worked for Lark. Lark made him work hard sometimes, but Lark was his brother and took care of him, and besides that, Tommy liked the animals: the horses and the cows. He wouldn't like to have to work in a kitchen. He walked around to the side of the building and looked in at another window. This time he found the lounge. There were lots of people in there. Some of them were eating, but most of them were just drinking. He saw some of the people who had come to town with the bad old man, and he saw the sheriff, Mr. Dort. Mr. Dort was standing at the door with his arms folded across his chest, and he looked like he was just watching things. Tommy wondered if Mr. Dort was expecting trouble, and he wondered, if that was the case, just what kind of trouble Mr. Dort was looking for.

There were so many people in there that it took him a long time to look them over, to look at their faces, and some of them had their backs to him, so it was hard to tell who they were. Finally he was satisfied that the bad old man wasn't one of the people he could see. He knew the room was bigger, though, that if he moved up closer to the window he'd be able to see more of them. Still, he didn't want anyone to see him there pressing his face against the window. He looked up at the sky and saw that it was getting dull and gray. It would be dark pretty soon, he figured. He would wait. He put his back against the wall of the building a few feet away from the window and sat down in the dirt. The knife in its scabbard pressed hard against his thigh, and he had to shift its position so he could sit there comfortably.

He would get through with his ugly task this evening, he thought. He would be glad to have it over with. He didn't like killing these people, but they were bad. They had hurt that young woman. He had seen it. The two men had taken her away somewhere and had cut off her hands and cut out her tongue. He had seen the stumps and he had seen the blood. And they had done other bad things to her, things that Lark and Spud didn't think he knew about. But he did know about them, and he knew that they had done those things to her. And the black man and that other woman, they had told the two men what to do and helped them do it and then they had laughed about it and teased the woman after she had been hurt. People shouldn't do those things to anyone, Tommy thought, but especially not to a pretty, helpless young woman. He had getten those four, but the bad old man was left. He was the one who had finally killed the woman. Now Tommy was going to kill him.

The sun had gone down a little lower and the sky was a heavy gray. Tommy stood up and inched his way to the window. Standing slightly to one side, he pressed his face against the rough siding of the building and peered in sideways. He could see more people than before. He knew there would be more. He looked from one face to another, and finally he saw him. His back was to the window, but Tommy could tell who he was. He was a big man, and he had wild white hair that fell clear to his shoulders. It was the bad old man. But the room was full of people and Mr. Dort still stood in the doorway. He had to find a way to get the bad old man out of the room, or to get the other people out of there. He sat down again to think.

Absent-mindedly he felt the matches in his shirt pocket. Lark didn't like for him to have them. He had sneaked them out of the match safe, the pretty tin box, where Dora kept them beside the stove. He liked the way their red tips flared up when they were scratched on a rough surface, so sometimes, even though he knew that it would make Lark mad at him, he sneaked some. Then it came to him. He knew how to get them out of the hotel. He clambered to his feet and ran back to the street behind the Railhead, turned, and hurried down to the other end of the street to the back of the stable. He looked inside. He could see no one. He tried the back door and found it unlocked. Inside, he opened all the stalls and chased the horses up close to the front of the building, then opened the front door so they could get out. Then he ran to the back of the building again, and dropped down on his knees. The floor was covered with loose straw, dry and ready to burn. He struck a match.

Pete Elston was Chief of the Pullman Voluntary Fire Department. He was proud of his position, and he was especially proud of the new steamer the town had purchased. It had never yet been used, not for a real fire, and Pete was secretly ecstatic when he heard the cry "Fire!" At last he would be able to get the new machine out and put it into action. It was a Hurp steam pumper with pumps under the driver's seat capable of pumping 600 gallons of water a minute. A man on the rear platform of the wagon stoked the boiler to create the steam to build up the pressure to operate the pumps. The latest thing. The best available. It was painted red and pulled by two white horses, and the blood seemed to race through Pete's veins as the white horses raced down the street toward the blazing stable. The bell was clanging, and people were running in the street alongside the steamer while the flames rose higher and grew hotter at the stable. Pete Elston shouted out orders, but they could not be heard over the general din.

Tommy Wheeler watched the excitement for a moment from the corner of the Railhead. Then he pulled himself away, for he remembered that he had something much more important to take care of. The fire was just to help him do his job. He was glad to see, though, that the horses had all run out the front of the stable to escape the blaze. He ran around the building and came up to the window he had looked through before. The room was empty. Tommy felt panic grip his insides. Why had he not realized that the bad old man would run out with everyone else? Where could he have gone? Tommy ran to the front of the building again and searched the crowd racing by in the street. All seemed utter confusion. It seemed as if the entire population was out on the street racing toward the fire. Tommy reached into his pocket and found his remaining matches. He thought hard, then turned and ran for the opposite end of town.

Adrian Channing's wagons were parked on the south side of the big theater which Tiff Lanagan called his opry house. Tommy grabbed the tongue of the wagon out front, turned it, and dragged the wagon until it was right up against the side of the building. Then he crawled inside the wagon from the rear and piled up all the cloth he could find. He struck a match and started a new fire. When he was satisfied that it would burn, he scrambled out of the wagon, ran to the back of the building, and hid himself around the corner. The flames were soon licking at the side of the theater.

Down at the stable Pete Elston's steamer was not making a good showing. The boiler wasn't hot enough to produce enough steam to develop the necessary pressure. The water pouring out the end of the hose was running uselessly onto the ground. People were running for buckets and forming a bucket brigade at the nozzle of the hose. Elston continued to shout unheeded orders while the fire roared. Horses ran wild in the street, and Jerry Slayton ran to and fro doing absolutely nothing worthwhile. Then someone in the crowd saw the flames from the other end of the street.

"Fire!" he shouted.

No one paid any attention. They already knew about the fire. He realized that, and shouted again.

"The opry house is burning. There's another fire."

A few heads turned. One was that of Adrian Channing.

"My wagons," he said, and he started down the street at a run. By the time Channing reached the theater, he was breathing hard and running more slowly. He had no water. No one had run to the theater with him. He rounded the corner of the building and saw his wagon in a blaze. Pulling off his jacket, he ran to the wagon and began beating at the flames.

Colfax and Lark Wheeler saw the flames before they would have been able to see the town without them. It was as if there were two extra sunsets, but in the wrong part of the sky. In surprise and confusion, they reined in their mounts.

"What the hell is that?" said Wheeler.

"It's Pullman," said Colfax. "Burning from both ends."

It was the time between daylight and darkness, that time of day when, more than any other time except its direct opposite, the dawn, the light plays tricks on vision. Colfax knew that it would be dangerous to race the horses pell-mell down the trail. Also, the distance was too great to run the horses hard the whole way, yet the flames created in Colfax, and apparently in Wheeler as well, an even greater sense of urgency than before.

"Let's go," said Wheeler, and he lashed his horse with the reins. Colfax, in spite of his better judgment, kicked his mount and shouted a command in order to keep pace with the other rider.

Adrian Channing could feel the flames singe his hair. His face was burning hot, yet he continued to beat at the inferno that raged inside his wagon and up the side of the theater building. *Where are the others?* he thought to himself. *Am I the only human being in this town who has seen these flames?* He slapped again, and as he drew back the jacket, now smoldering, for another swing, a flaming piece of wagon cover came with it, came at him, and he dodged it with an involuntary cry. As he stepped back and aside, he tripped and fell heavily to his back. There on the ground, forced to pause, his mind took quick stock of his hopeless situation. Four of his actors were dead, and the wagon was a loss. He knew in that instant that he was fighting a losing battle. He raised himself up on his elbows and watched. He was giving it up. He was finished.

Then from around the far side of the flaming wagon came Tommy Wheeler, knife held high. Channing screamed again as he rolled quickly to one side, just in time to avoid Tommy's wild thrust. Tommy landed on his belly, his knife buried in the earth where Channing had been. Both men scrambled to their feet. Channing assumed the defensive posture of a wrestler. His eyes were opened wide, and the light from the nearby flames danced across his old features, making hideous patterns.

"Listen to me," he said, his voice coming with difficulty

through his heavy breathing. "Listen, Tommy. It was only a play. No one was hurt."

"I saw you," said Tommy, and he raised the knife high above his head and lunged for Channing. The old man caught the arm that swung the knife in both his hands, then turned, throwing his backside into Tommy's smaller much lighter body. He thrust with his hips and pulled with his arms, and Tommy went flying through the air over the old man's shoulders. Tommy shouted as he flew, but the shout ended when he landed on his back with a hard thud and the wind went out of his lungs and he dropped the knife. He lay on his back, gasping for breath, and only a few paces away Channing stood. Channing knew that he should make another move, take advantage of his temporary upper hand, but the physical exertion of the whole evening had taken its toll. He felt his age more acutely than he ever had before. He was breathing heavily, his shoulders and chest moving in great, desperate heaves. He tried to move, but he couldn't seem to lift his foot. He watched as Tommy tried to get back his breath, and he prayed that his strength would return before that happened.

Then Tommy rolled over and got himself up to his hands and knees. He groped in the dirt for his knife. Channing took desperate deep breaths and braced himself for another rush. Tommy found the knife, grasped it, and stood up. But he didn't rush Channing. He had done that before, and the old man had thrown him. He was more wary. He held the knife out in front of him and began to circle his prey. He reached out tentatively toward Channing with the blade a couple of times, and Channing reacted with defensive moves. Tommy saw that this one was not going to be as easy as the other four. He was frightened, but it was too late to change his mind. It had to be done now. There wouldn't be another chance. He lowered the knife and rushed Channing with a swift uppercutting motion, the tip of the blade aimed low toward Channing's gut. Again the old man reacted quickly, grabbing Tommy's wrist. The point of the blade stabbed into Channing's thigh, but only an inch or so deep. He held Tommy's wrist in a viselike grip. With his free hand, Tommy reached up to grab a handful of white hair and began pulling Channing's head to one side. Channing growled like an old bear. Gripping Tommy's wrist as hard as he could with his left hand, he released the grip of his right and dealt Tommy a stunning blow to the side of his head. Tommy staggered backward, and as he did, Channing released his wrist. But the force of the blow caused the old man to drop forward to his knees. He tried to rise, but he could not find the strength. Tommy recovered himself from the blow to his head and stepped around behind the kneeling figure of the actor. He raised his knife high in the air.

"Tommy."

The voice came cutting through the hot night air like something solid.

Tommy stood still, his arm raised high. He looked in the direction of the voice that had called his name. There beside the blazing wagon, Colfax stood, his right arm extended before him, the big Colt in his hand. Tommy looked at the face of Colfax, demonic in the red glare of the flames. Then he looked at the barrel of the big Colt. It was pointed directly at his chest.

"Tommy," said Colfax, "it's all over. Drop the knife."

Tommy stood still and stared. His eyes were opened wide in fright and confusion. He had heard his brothers and other men talk about this killing man. He had heard them say that no one had ever escaped Colfax once he got on the trail, and now Colfax was pointing his gun at Tommy. Did Colfax like the bad old man? Tommy had thought that Colfax liked him and his brothers. He didn't understand.

"No," he said. "He's the bad man. He hurt the lady."

"Tommy," said Colfax as he thumbed back the hammer of the Colt, "put down the knife. Then we'll talk about this. Put it down."

"No."

Tommy turned and ran into the darkness. Colfax followed the fleeing figure with his Colt. He had a bead on Tommy's back, and he felt his finger tightening on the trigger. Then suddenly he bent his elbow and released the hammer. He holstered the Colt and stepped quickly to Channing's side.

"Mr. Channing," he said, "are you all right?"

Channing was still breathing heavily and had difficulty answering Colfax.

"I'm afraid," he said, "that I'm—not as young—as I used to be. The fire—and the fight—have utterly—worn me out."

"Can you stand?"

Colfax put Channing's arm around his shoulders and helped him to his feet.

"Hadn't you—better—go after that—young man?" said Channing.

"Not until I get you to a safe and comfortable place," said Colfax. "Come on."

The Railhead was a safe distance from the flames of either the stable or the theater, and Colfax walked Channing into its lounge, got him seated, and went behind the bar to get him a shot of brandy. No one else was inside, the fires having attracted every able-bodied man in Pullman. He poured the brandy and took the glass to Channing.

"Here," he said. "Drink this."

Channing took a sip of the brandy and coughed. He caught his breath and took another sip.

"I'll be all right,' he said. "Thank you. You came just in the nick of time, you know. If you hadn't come, I'd be a corpse by now for sure."

He turned up the glass and finished the brandy. Colfax picked up the glass and stood.

"You want another one?" he asked.

"Well, yes," said Channing. "One more just might put me in tip-top shape again. God, I hope I never have to do that again. I'm past my prime, you know, and I've long since surpassed my fighting weight."

Colfax brought the bottle back from the bar and sat down again with Channing. He refilled Channing's glass.

"You're not going after young Wheeler?" asked Channing.

"I'm not leaving you here alone until he's been caught," said Colfax. "Not for a minute."

When Tommy Wheeler ran from Colfax, he went around the corner to the front of the theater. He looked down the main street of Pullman and saw the blaze of the stable at the other end of town. Most of the citizenry were still down there, shouting and rushing about, but they were beginning to get the fire under control, and a few of them had turned to start toward the theater. Tommy ran toward them for a confused moment, then turned and ran between two buildings. He stopped there in the dark to gather his thoughts. He wondered where Lark was. Lark would help him. Lark would be mad at him, but he would help him. He always did. Lark was probably at home. Tommy wanted to be home. Then he remembered where he had left his horse, and he ran for the back street he had come into town on. Reaching the street, he turned and ran for his horse. He saw it down there in the dark, a large shadowy shape. He would soon be on his way home. He was close to the horse before he noticed the other shape there, the shape of a man standing beside the horse, a man with a rifle in his hand. Tommy stopped. His heart was pounding furiously in his chest. Then he recognized the man, and he smiled.

"Lark," he said.

Lark Wheeler raised the rifle and pulled the trigger. The bullet tore into Tommy's chest, just above the sternum and slightly to the left. Tommy stood still, his mouth opened in amazement. He looked down at the wound in his chest. It was gushing blood. He dropped his knife and placed both hands over the spouting hole, and the blood ran freely between his fingers and down the front of his shirt. He looked up again at his brother.

"Lark?" he said, and his eyes glazed over and his face went blank and expressionless and he fell forward like a tree that has just been felled.

Chapter Nineteen

It was late. The flames were out, but there was nothing left of either Jerry Slayton's stable or Tiff Lanagan's opry house but smoldering ashes. The lounge in the Railhead was having a remarkably good night, as everyone seemed to be too excited from the events of the evening to go home to bed. Lark Wheeler had taken his brother's body and left town as soon as Sheriff Dort had been apprised of all the necessary details. He had also told Colfax that he and what remained of his family would be moving on. Colfax himself felt a tremendous sense of relief. Both jobs were done. The murder case had probably been the single worst experience of his life, and he was glad to have it all behind him. He felt free again, and he was having a few drinks of brandy with Adrian Channing and what was left of Channing's traveling theatrical company. He had enough cash from Lanagan to allow him some relaxing time. He would get drunk, and when he had slept it off, he would buy a ticket on the next train to Texas. He wanted badly to see Bluff Luton, although he couldn't exactly say why.

Boyd Gruver was at the bar. He had come into town with other cowboys from Lanagan's ranch when they had seen the flames. He tossed down a shot of whiskey and walked over to the table at which Colfax was seated with Channing, Alma, and the other actors.

"Colfax," he said.

Colfax turned to look at Gruver.

"I didn't like you at first," said Gruver. "I admit you took some getting used to. But, well, you done what you said you'd do, and I got to admit, you're a hell of a man. I'd like to shake your hand."

Colfax stared at Gruver for a moment, then looked away.

"I still don't like you, Mr. Gruver," he said. "I don't like you and I don't like your boss. I don't like the way you do things."

Gruver thought about making a response, then thought better of it, turned, and left the lounge.

"Weren't you a little hard on him?" said Alma.

"I don't think so," said Colfax. "I watched them hang a man."

"Well," said Channing, "I'm afraid that I must turn in. It's been a very rough day for an old man."

"What will you do from here, Mr. Channing?" asked Colfax.

"I'll take what's left of my people in my remaining wagons and return to New York. It's all I can do. Once there, I'll start over."

"I wish you good luck," said Colfax. "Meeting you has been a great pleasure, although I certainly regret the circumstances surrounding the meeting."

"Mr. Colfax," said Channing, "those circumstances would in all probability have been much worse had you not been here. I'm deeply in your debt. Good night, sir."

With Channing gone, the other actors soon finished their drinks and excused themselves. Colfax found himself alone with Alma Dyer. He poured himself another drink and offered one to Alma.

"No, thanks," she said. "I would like a cigarette."

He reached into his pocket and offered her the makings, then watched with fascination as she rolled herself a smoke. He handed her the matchbox from inside his vest pocket, and he smiled as she lit her cigarette.

"You are a remarkable woman, Alma," he said.

"What? Because I can roll a cigarette?"

"Yes. You can roll cigarette. You can act. You are brilliant and you are beautiful."

Colfax had never before in his life said those kinds of things to a woman. He was a bit surprised at himself, but he knew that the brandy had loosened his tongue. He was glad of it. He tossed down his drink and poured himself another. Alma took a deep drag off her cigarette and exhaled a cloud of smoke.

"I believe that I would like another drink," she said.

Colfax poured her drink. Then he rolled himself a cigarette and lit it.

"What about you?" she said.

"What?"

"What now? Will you go to Texas?"

"Yes, I will. Right now I'm going to get drunk, but later, after I've slept, I will go to Texas. On the next train. Are you going back to New York City with Mr. Channing?"

"I don't know, Cole."

Colfax took another drink. His head was beginning to feel light, but he liked the feeling, and, what was more, he needed it for what he was going to say.

"Would you like to see Texas?" he said. Alma sipped at her brandy.

"Yes," she said.

Colfax leaned his elbows on the table and looked directly into Alma's face.

"Would you—accompany me—on the train to Texas?" he said. He noticed that asking the question—forming the words and forcing them to escape from his mouth—had increased his heartbeat. Alma shifted her eyes without turning her head so that she was looking into his. They stared into each other's eyes for what seemed a long moment. She reached across the table and put a hand on top of his.

"Yes," she said. "I'd like that. Very much. I was beginning to think that you wouldn't ask."